COLIN'S FANTASTIC
VIDEO ADVENTURE

COLIN'S FANTASTIC VIDEO ADVENTURE

by Kenneth Oppel

illustrated by Kathleen C. Howell

E. P. DUTTON   NEW YORK

Text copyright © 1985 by Kenneth Oppel
Illustrations copyright © 1985 by Kathleen C. Howell

Library of Congress Cataloging in Publication Data

Oppel, Kenneth.
   Colin's fantastic video adventure.

   Summary: Eleven-year-old Colin discovers that the
spaceships in his favorite video game are actually
controlled by tiny men who promise to help him in an
upcoming contest.
   1. Children's stories, Canadian. [1. Video games—
Fiction. 2. Science fiction] I. Howell, Kathleen C.,
ill. II. Title.
PZ7.0614Co 1985 [Fic] 84-25911
ISBN 0-525-44151-4

Published in the United States by E. P. Dutton, Inc.,
2 Park Avenue, New York, N.Y. 10016

Editor: Julie Amper   Designer: Isabel Warren-Lynch

Printed in the U.S.A.   OBE   First Edition
10 9 8 7 6 5 4 3 2 1

to Silvia

Contents

Out of Order

Colin Filmore was sitting in math class, waiting.

He looked at his watch. In two minutes, school would be out for the week. At the moment, this meant only one thing to Colin. It meant that he would soon be playing Meteoroids.

Meteoroids is not one of those games where you roll dice and move little plastic figures around a board. Those games are boring—even more so than staring at the ceiling or waiting for your fingernails to grow.

Meteoroids is a coin-operated video game. It is a large boxlike structure about the size of a refrigerator. There is a television screen on the front of the game, and underneath is a ledge. On this ledge are the joystick and several buttons. After you slip your coin into the slot and press the START button, you are in command of a little spaceship that travels at awesome speed among the stars, shooting laser bullets at gigantic meteoroids and enemy flying saucers.

Colin was absolutely bonkers about Meteoroids, and he played it every day after school. During geography period, he had thought up a new strategy for exploding outer-space rocks. He was anxious to try it out.

"Right, then," said Mr. Talbot, the math teacher, turning to face the class. "Will you please focus your attention on the problem I have just written on the board? How many pins, each three inches long, will fit inside a hollow cube with sides of thirteen yards?"

The bell rang.

All the students sprang out of their seats as if propelled by powerful springs. Colin snatched the books off his desk and made a run for the door, far ahead of his classmates.

"Colin Filmore!" shrieked the teacher. He had a very shrill voice for a man. "Where the heck do you think you're going?"

"The bell rang, sir," Colin said.

"*What* bell?" Mr. Talbot asked. "I didn't hear any bell! Did you hear a bell?" he growled, pointing a long finger at a small boy.

"No, Mr. Talbot," said the boy, trembling with fear.

"You see!" the math teacher cried triumphantly. A mad little spark blazed in each of his eyes now. "Sit down, Mr. Filmore. Sit down, all of you."

As Colin returned to his desk, he knew that Mr. Talbot was going to be nasty.

Mr. Talbot stood quietly, looking from one person to another with his fiery eyes. He was holding a piece of chalk in his hand.

"Now," he said suddenly, making everyone in the room jump, "I asked you people a question that you have neglected to answer. And I think it is only right that Mr. Filmore answer it."

Oh, no, Colin thought.

The math teacher sat down on the stool beside his desk and didn't take his eyes off Colin.

Concentrate, Colin told himself. You've got to think hard to solve a problem like this. Now, I know that the pin is three inches long, but how thick is it? And is it all one thickness? Surely the top is thicker than the pointed end!

Mr. Talbot began to sigh loudly and make clucking noises with his tongue. Then he started throwing the piece of chalk high up in the air and catching it.

It's impossible, Colin thought. It can't be solved. How on earth does he expect me to find how many pins will fit in the box when I don't even know the exact size of the pin?

Up went the chalk. Mr. Talbot caught it, sighed, clucked, and threw it up again. This time, however, the toss was a bad one. The chalk started coming down behind the teacher's head. He leaned back on his stool and tried to catch it. He had leaned too far. He had lost his balance! Mr. Talbot fell from the stool, and his head clunked on the hard concrete floor. Mr. Talbot was out cold.

Someone went to tell the principal.

Math class was obviously over. Colin rushed out of the room and down the crowded corridor. He stopped at his locker to collect some books he would need over the weekend. Then he raced out the main doors.

Colin headed toward Mr. Schmidt's delicatessen, across the road from the school field. Mr. Schmidt kept a Meteoroids game in a corner of the room, beside the shelves of imported spices. Colin knew that within ten minutes, many kids from school would be crowded around the game, waiting impatiently for their turns. He quickened

kathleen c. howell

his pace, breaking into a jog. He wanted to be first.

The small bell above the door jangled as he burst into the delicatessen. Mr. Schmidt, a tall and skinny man, was sitting behind the counter, reading a book. It was titled *How To Make Big Bucks in One Heck of a Hurry*.

"Hi, Colin," he mumbled.

"Hello, Mr. Schmidt," Colin said. "Did you lose your watch?" he asked, looking at the owner's bare wrist.

"I was playing poker last night," Mr. Schmidt said.

"Oh," said Colin. "I see." He walked down to the end of the shop and dropped his books to the floor beside the Meteoroids game. He slipped a quarter into the coin slot and went over his new strategy one last time.

Then he pressed the START button and gripped the joystick tightly.

The delicatessen was filled with a harsh whirring noise. It was coming from inside the game. There was a bright flash of light from the television screen that made Colin blink and look away. When he looked back, the screen had turned dark.

"Perfect!" cried Mr. Schmidt, throwing down his book and walking toward the game. "I knew the beastly machine would break down at a bad time!"

He went to the cash register and gave Colin a quarter in exchange for the one he had put in the coin slot. Then, in large letters, he wrote OUT OF ORDER on a piece of paper and taped it to the blank screen of the game.

Snogel and Drogel

When he got home, Colin took the key to the door from underneath a flat rock in the garden and went inside. In the kitchen, he put his knapsack on the table and fixed himself a snack: a glass of milk, two chocolate-chip cookies, and an apple. He carried all this into the living room and flopped on the sofa. With the remote-control unit, he switched on the television set.

"I simply cannot believe it!" an enormously fat lady was squealing. She had just won a new car on a game show. "I just can't believe it! Is this wonderful thing *really* mine?"

"It certainly is, Miss Gargantua," said the host, smiling a sickeningly sweet smile.

"It just boggles the mind!" cried the lady. She started hugging the host and giving him large, wet kisses on the cheeks.

Colin snapped the TV off in disgust.

As he sat there on the couch, feeling let down because of the broken Meteoroids game, he thought he heard faint noises in the house. It was as if people were whispering to one another. Colin held his breath and listened. He heard the same sort of sound again, this time louder. He let his breath out sharply. It could not be his mother and father. She was showing people around the city, trying to sell expensive houses; he was giving people legal advice in his cushy office downtown. Colin didn't have any brothers or sisters.

At this point, he was getting jumpy. People a lot older than Colin get jumpy when they're alone in the house and hear strange noises, so there is no reason why he shouldn't have been scared out of his skin.

In fact, he wasn't. He was about to get off the sofa and seek out the owners of these annoying voices, when he heard a distinct exclamation that made him freeze.

"You're taking up too much room, stupid!" the voice screamed. A tingling bolt of electricity ran down Colin's neck to his feet, not because of *what* he had heard— that really wasn't very alarming—but because of *where* it had come from.

It had come from his *shirt pocket!*

Cautiously, he pulled the flap of the pocket away from his body and looked inside. There he saw the helmeted heads of two very tiny men. The two men were looking right up at Colin, their eyes wide, their mouths gaping slightly. Colin looked at them some more, and the miniature men looked back.

"Oh, *now* look what you've done," moaned one of the little men, clutching his helmeted head. "If you had only been quiet."

"Silence!" shouted the other, glaring at his companion. "This is all your fault! You were standing on my foot, and your elbow was jammed into my stomach. I never should have agreed to your silly plan!"

The man clutching his helmet looked at Colin. "If you would be so kind . . . if you would be so kind as to get us out of here."

Colin nodded and carefully reached down into his pocket and brought out the diminutive men, placing them gently on the coffee table.

Now that they were out of his pocket, Colin could see them more clearly. Both were wearing what looked like space suits, and on their feet they wore sneakers. Black gauntlets covered their hands. One of the little men was tall and slim. The other was slightly shorter and quite stout. They had taken off their bubblelike helmets and were holding them at their sides.

"Who are you two?" Colin asked. His mouth had gone dry, and he reached for his glass of milk and took a small sip.

"I am Drogel," the taller of the two said. "And this is—"

"Snogel," interrupted the stout man.

Colin looked above their heads, searching carefully for fine strands of thread. Perhaps these little people were marionettes.

"What are you doing?" Snogel asked.

"Looking for wires," Colin replied.

"Don't be idiotic," said Snogel. "We're as real as you are."

"Where did you come from?" Colin asked.

"Hmmmmm," Drogel said.

"Ahhhhh," Snogel said.

They looked at each other apprehensively for several moments. Obviously, the two men were reluctant to say anything. Then Drogel shrugged his shoulders and looked up at Colin.

Colin swallowed and prepared himself for what he was about to hear.

"Well," Drogel began, chewing on his fingernails beneath dark gloves, "we came from . . . er . . . we came from . . . ah . . . the game."

"How's that?"

"We came from the game, Meteoroids," said Snogel. "You see, we are the pilots of the spaceship." He said this proudly and thrust out his tiny chest.

"Impossible!" said Colin, absolutely flabbergasted. "It's all wiring and computer chips. It's just a complex machine!"

"Machine, is it?" Snogel snapped. "Machine! A simple machine? My dear overgrown boy, there's more to that game than you know!"

"There certainly is," agreed Drogel, grinning. "Who do you think *really* controls the spaceship? Not you!"

Colin took a deep breath and tried to collect his thoughts. "Now look," he began slowly, "what you are telling me can't possibly be true. That ship on the television screen is only an image! How could you *fit* inside a picture?"

"Ah," said Drogel, his small eyes twinkling. "That's it, isn't it! You have hit right on it! What a clever lad you are. Now, if you would like, I'll explain the whole thing to you."

"I'd like that very much," Colin said, tingling all over.

The Fantastic Level

Drogel set his helmet on the coffee table and sat down on it. "You see," he said, his voice softening as voices often do when they are about to reveal great secrets, "everything you watch on the television screen is *actually happening*, not inside the game, but on some fantastic level. So as soon as Snogel and I enter Meteoroids, we are whisked away into another world!"

"You mean that you and Snogel are really flying a spaceship through meteoroid fields and fighting with enemy ships?" Colin asked.

"Exactly!" Drogel said. "What is your name, by the way?"

"Colin Filmore. And you are saying that I am seeing only a representation of what is going on in this fantastic level?"

"You astound me!" Drogel said.

"So I really don't do anything at all," Colin said, disappointed. "It's you two who do all the work."

"No, no," corrected the tall but tiny man. "We do only what *you* tell us to, by way of the joystick and buttons. So if you press the button that says ACCELERATION, we speed up until you take your finger off that button. In our ship, we have a huge panel above our heads that we watch constantly. Everything you do is registered there. It's really quite simple."

"*Not* so simple!" shouted Snogel. "How can you say that, Drogel? It's darn terrifying! When you play the game, my overlarge boy, you know that it's just a game, and you can more or less have a relaxed time. In the cockpit, it's frantic. We're both watching that flashing panel above us and flipping toggle switches right, left, and center. We get pulverized by rocks and blown to smithereens by those wretched flying saucers. And then, somehow, it starts all over again. In one way or another, we must get smashed over a hundred times in a single day! There's nothing we can do about it either! Our job is simply to obey the commands of the player. I am a bundle of nerves! And I'll tell you what's worst of all. It's when little children of five or six get a quarter from Mummy and slip it into the game without even knowing how to play! Some can't even reach the joystick! It's a massacre then, I'll tell you that much!"

Drogel looked at his companion in awe.

"That was very impressive, Snogel. I love it when you get angry. It's terrific!"

"Thank you, Drogel."

"To be perfectly honest," Drogel said to Colin, "it *is* rather hectic, and that's why we left the game. We're in need of a good vacation."

"Vacation!" Colin exclaimed.

"Yes, of course," said Drogel indignantly. "We have to take breaks, too, you know. We're people, too! Besides, Snogel was on the verge of a nervous breakdown."

"And look what's happened," Snogel complained,

pointing at Colin. "Now we've been discovered by a young brat just because you wanted to hitch a ride instead of walking. We could have been at the beach by now."

"The beach?" Colin said.

"Yes," said Drogel. "I hear it's lovely in April."

"Look," said Colin, "slow down. How did you get *out* of the game and into my shirt pocket?"

"First of all," Drogel explained, "there are two exits from the fantastic level. One is through the television screen; the other is through a small concealed door at the back of the game. In our cockpit, there are two special buttons. One says EXIT ONE, the other says EXIT TWO. When we press one of them, *whoosh*, we're out. EXIT ONE puts us right through the screen. That's the one we used with you, so we could hide in your pocket."

Colin gave Drogel a long, hard stare.

"What's wrong?" he asked.

"These things are hard to believe," Colin replied.

Drogel shrugged. "I'm sure that in the sixteenth century, people had a hard time believing Copernicus when he told them that the Earth wasn't the center of the universe. As well, the Greek astronomer Eratosthenes was probably laughed at twenty-two hundred years ago, when he discovered that the world was not flat but round. You see, my dear Colin, there are many things people have had trouble believing."

Silence.

"Were those real people, Drogel?" Snogel asked quietly.

"Of course they were *real* people!"

"All right," said Colin. "I'm sorry for having doubted you, but if you came right through the screen, why didn't I see you?"

13

"I'll handle this one," Snogel said. "My gigantic boy, if you will remember, the screen flashed, and you blinked and turned your face away. That gave us more than enough time to dive into your pocket."

"I'd forgotten," admitted Colin. "What will happen to the game, now that you're gone?"

"Good heavens, you ask a lot of questions!" Drogel exclaimed. "Mr. Schmidt will call a repairman who will bring along another pair of pilots."

"The repairmen know about you?" Colin cried.

"No, no," said Drogel. "Whenever a game breaks down, the repairman brings along two very large computer chips. He takes out the old chips and puts in the new ones. He hasn't the slightest idea that in each of these chips is a pilot. After that, the two pilots enter the fantastic level, and the game is back in working order. Only the president of the game company knows about us. It's an extremely well-kept secret, though. You are the very first outside person to learn about us."

"Where in the world does the company find people like you?"

Drogel ran a gloved hand through his hair and looked at Snogel. Snogel scratched his cheek and looked back at his taller companion. Then there was a whispered conference.

"Haven't the foggiest idea!" announced Drogel.

Colin took a long drink of milk and sat back in the sofa. He was trying to remain calm while letting all these facts sink in. "Would I be right," he began slowly, tracing a circle on his glass with a finger, "if I said that Meteoroids was the *only* video game with pilots inside?"

"Holy halibut, no!" Drogel laughed. "Listen very carefully, my boy. *Every single coin-operated video game has* controllers *like us who work on that fantastic level!*"

"You're serious?"

"Yes," replied Snogel.

"Very," added Drogel.

Colin looked from one little man to the other, each smiling reassuringly at him.

"Incredible," Colin said, shaking his head. "This whole thing is incredible. My mom and dad will go nuts when I tell them about you two."

"Holy hologram!" cried Drogel. "You mustn't ever tell them about us!"

"Why not?"

"For one thing," Drogel answered, "we're supposed to be kept secret. If you go and tell your parents, they will either not believe you at all or go to the papers. That would be the end of us. There would be a thousand old scientists poking their noses into the scene. You must promise us never to tell, Colin."

"All right," the youth said. He certainly did not want to do anything that would make their lives miserable.

Just then, a car pulled up in the driveway.

"Look, you two," Colin said, "my mother's just come home. You've got to hide, or she'll see you! Get your helmets!"

He picked up the two space pilots and rushed them upstairs to his bedroom. He pulled open a drawer full of clothes. "Stay in here," he instructed.

"Well, I never!" exclaimed Snogel. "A drawer!"

"Actually, it is quite comfortable," murmured Drogel, stretching out on a pair of socks.

"And what about our vacation, eh?" shouted Snogel. "We should be at the beach!"

"Be quiet. I'll get you out later," Colin said, and he closed the drawer.

16

The Brilliant Idea

"Mr. Talbot knocked himself out today in class," Colin said. He was having dinner with his parents.

"Really?" Mr. Filmore asked, looking up from his plate.

"Uh-huh. He fell right off his stool and hit his head on the floor."

"Was the stool defective?" asked Mr. Filmore. An eager gleam had come into his eyes, and he was leaning toward Colin across the dinner table. "And if so, what was the name of the company that made it? There could be an absolutely super-duper lawsuit over this one!"

"There was nothing wrong with the stool, Dad," said Colin. "Mr. Talbot was throwing his chalk in the air and catching it. I've told you how he does that when he wants to make somebody in the class feel uncomfortable. This time, he lost his balance while making a grab for the chalk."

"Oh," Mr. Filmore said, sinking back in his chair.

"I think Mr. Talbot is an idiot," Mrs. Filmore said. "At the last parent-teacher meeting, he said it was essential that he have absolute control over the minds of his students."

"He's gone off his track all right," Colin said.

"Did anything else interesting happen today, Colin?" his mother asked.

Yes, Colin wanted to say. Yes, something else interesting *did* happen today. Two tiny men—and by tiny, I mean about three or four inches tall—found their way into my shirt pocket. Right at this moment, they are hiding in a drawer in my room, waiting to take a vacation.

"No," said Colin. "Besides what happened to Mr. Talbot, it was a very normal sort of day." He finished his meal and excused himself from the table.

In his bedroom, Colin lay on his bed so that he was able to look out the window. This window was very tall, and it ran down almost the whole length of the wall. Colin found that he could always think better when he was looking through a window. It was the middle of April, and the days were becoming longer. Even though it was close to eight o'clock, Colin could see, over the garage roof, the sun hovering above the horizon. The wind breezing into his bedroom was cool and smelled of fresh-cut grass.

At the moment, Colin was thinking about what he should do with the two pilots in his drawer. He decided that there was really only one fair thing to do. He would wait until his parents were asleep, and then he would let Snogel and Drogel out so they could get on with their vacation. And that would be the end of it.

He watched a movie on TV at eight. Then he read an electronics magazine for half an hour. After that, Colin changed into his pajamas, turned off the lights, and crawled into bed.

By the time the lights in his parents' room had gone out, Colin was feeling quite drowsy, and he was worried that he would fall asleep before he could get Snogel and Drogel out. But he decided to wait at least fifteen more minutes just to be safe.

Then a strange thing happened. While Colin was trying hard to stay awake, an idea drifted into his mind. It simply flowed right into his head without his even thinking, and it was fantastic. Actually, it was not only a fantastic idea but an outrageously brilliant idea. It was the kind geniuses get on good days, and other people get maybe ten times in a lifetime. Now Colin was so excited that he couldn't have gone to sleep if he had tried.

He had to tell Drogel and Snogel about his idea immediately. He got out of bed, closed the door, went over to his desk, and turned on a small lamp. He then opened the drawer. There they were, sleeping.

"Wake up," Colin whispered, "wake up."

This didn't work. Colin decided more drastic measures were needed. He walked into his small bathroom and picked up a glass. He turned on one of the taps and waited until the water coming out was good and cold. Then he filled the glass halfway with water and went back to the open drawer. He poured the water all over the two tiny men.

"Who . . . what!" shouted Drogel.

"Where . . . when!" cried Snogel.

"Sh-h-h!" hissed Colin.

"You devilish little brat!" Snogel gasped. "What's the big idea of dousing us with icy water?"

"I had to wake you up," Colin said.

"What time is it?" asked Drogel, trying his best to brush water off his soaking space suit.

Colin looked at the digital clock on his night table. "It's almost eleven thirty."

"Wake us up?" Snogel said, incredulous. "At eleven thirty at night?"

"I had to wake you up," Colin said again. "I *was* going to set you on your way to the beach, but I've come up with an idea, and I have to tell you about it. It's rather incredible."

"Well," said Snogel grumpily, "now that we're wide-awake, you may as well tell us. But first, take us out of here and put us under that lamp so we can dry off."

Colin lifted the minuscule men out of the drawer and placed them on his desk. He twisted the neck of the lamp down so that the shade completely covered Snogel and Drogel. Colin could see their dark forms—one tall, the other stout—through the yellow plastic of the lampshade.

"Go ahead!" came Snogel's muffled voice.

"We're ready for it," Drogel said.

Colin took a deep breath before he allowed himself to begin.

"Even though you two obey the commands of the players, you are actually in total control of the space-ship. Right? Good, Now, the way I see it, if you wanted, you could operate that ship *all . . . by . . . yourselves!* You wouldn't even have to glance at the flashing panel of lights over your heads.

"You would obviously be excellent pilots because you've spent so much time in the cockpit. You know the movements of the ship. You would hardly ever get destroyed, and you would earn extremely high scores. And there are Meteoroids contests that give great prizes to the winner. My idea is this. We should work as a team,

entering every Meteoroids contest possible. When it comes time for me to take my turn, I'll slip you two into the game so that you can pilot the spaceship. I will simply make it *look* as if I am playing. The money we win would, of course, be split evenly among us. And if we win enough contests, you two could buy a large home in some luxurious tropical region of the world. So, what do you think?"

"Fantastic!" cried Drogel. He sounded enthralled.

"Horrible!" screeched Snogel. He was obviously aghast. "What do you mean, *fantastic*, you blithering fool? My nerves are frayed enough as it is. That would be pure torture."

"It would be lots of fun!" said Drogel. "It would be the first time we really piloted that ship. It would be . . . an adventure. A fantastic video adventure!"

"Well, what do you say, Snogel?" Colin asked.

"I say, get me out from underneath this light bulb. I'm cooking!"

"Wow," said Drogel as Colin lifted the lampshade away from the desktop, "I was getting quite a suntan in there."

"I would like to go back to sleep now," Snogel said.

"Come on, Snogel!" implored Colin.

"I'll think about it," the stout pilot said. "I'll tell you my decision tomorrow morning. It's Saturday tomorrow; no school for you brats. There should be school every day of the week, every month of the year."

"It's a fabulous idea, Colin," Drogel said as he was picked up and put into a dry drawer. "A brilliant idea!"

Breakfast

Colin woke up early the next morning.

He instantly remembered the amazing things that had taken place yesterday, and he lay still under his blankets and wondered if Snogel would go along with the plan. Colin realized that the plan would simply not work unless both space pilots were involved. He leapt out of bed and dressed quickly. He wanted to see if Snogel and Drogel were awake yet. Colin opened the drawer smoothly and slowly, in case they were sleeping. They were not. Snogel and Drogel were stretched out on a chessboard.

They were arm wrestling.

"You can't win, Drogel," grunted Snogel, who was losing.

"I have superior strength, my dear friend," gasped Drogel.

Neither of them noticed Colin.

"Oh, no!" panted Snogel. "I think my arm is about to snap clean off!"

"Don't be idiotic," puffed Drogel, slowly pushing down his friend's arm.

"I'm deadly serious," Snogel said. "I can feel it. I can feel my bones ready to snap in two. They're bending dangerously."

"Are you sure?" Drogel said, looking carefully at his friend, concern showing clearly on his narrow face. He loosened his tight hold on Snogel's hand and stopped pushing.

"It suddenly got better!" shouted Snogel. He took Drogel by surprise and nearly forced his arm all the way down.

"You tricked me!" exclaimed Drogel. He had to use all his strength just to hold his position.

Their foreheads were covered with perspiration.

"Good heavens!" said Drogel suddenly. "Snogel, what on earth *is* that vile creature slithering onto your shoulder?" He put on a shocked face.

Snogel's face turned a bit pale. "I can't feel a thing," he said softly.

"Of course not," said Drogel. "Of course you can't feel it through your thick space suit. Be careful. It looks like a Speckled Flywrangler to me."

"What should I do?" squeaked Snogel.

"First of all," instructed Drogel, "don't look at it. You would go mad from fright. Look straight ahead and remain perfectly still."

Snogel was so terrified that his arm went limp. It was easy for Drogel to win the arm wrestle.

"Is it gone yet?"

"It was never there, my brave companion," said Drogel, standing up.

"That was unforgivable! I hate it when you outsmart me!"

"Hello, Colin," said Drogel, looking up at the boy.

24

"Good morning," Colin greeted him. "Did you have a decent night's sleep?"

"As decent as it gets, sleeping on chessboards!" snapped Snogel. He was grumpy over having lost the arm wrestle.

Colin knew that the chances of Snogel's agreeing to go along with his plan would be much higher if he were in a better mood.

"You arm wrestle very well, Snogel," Colin said. "I was sure you were going to win."

"You don't have to flatter me," said Snogel. "I've decided that I'm going to do it."

"Great!" said Colin. "Terrific!"

"Just let me assure you, though, that I'm only doing it for the money."

"I think the first thing we should do," said Colin, talking fast, "is go to the delicatessen and see how well you can pilot the spaceship on your own. Mr. Schmidt won't have had the game fixed yet, and you can just slip back in. When do you want to start? Today? As soon as the delicatessen opens? It's always quietest in the mornings."

"My dear boy! Something is going to pop in your head if you don't slow down," Drogel warned. "Now, Snogel and I will go to the delicatessen and back into our game today as soon as you've had some breakfast. Breakfast is a very important meal for a growing child like yourself."

"Don't you two ever eat anything?" Colin asked.

"Actually, now that you mention it—" began Drogel.

"We most certainly do!" Snogel said. "It's just that with all the excitement around here lately, we have forgotten our mighty appetites. Bring me back toast with marmalade on it, if you please."

"Could you bring me an apple?" Drogel asked. "That would be fine."

"Mind you," Snogel went on, "the toast must be very dark. A piece of bread that is lightly toasted is totally unacceptable, I'm afraid."

"The apple should be green and peeled. I cannot digest the skin very well at all."

"Butter, not margarine. I find that vegetable products are upsetting to my stomach."

"If it's not too much trouble," Drogel said slowly, "could you slice the apple into small pieces?"

"And spread the marmalade in a thin layer over the toast."

Colin seized a small notepad and a pencil and began jotting down the two men's orders.

"You can come downstairs to the kitchen with me and help," Colin said.

"What about your parents?" Snogel asked.

"They don't get up until ten o'clock on the weekend. It'll be safe; we've got a good two hours."

With Colin leading the way, the three walked quietly along the upstairs hallway. When Snogel and Drogel reached the top of the staircase, they stopped.

"What's the matter?" Colin asked.

"These are pretty steep steps," Snogel answered.

"Do you want me to carry you down?" Colin said.

"No," said Snogel, "we can manage. Drogel, this calls for Method Number Three."

"Yes," Drogel agreed. "I think you're right."

"What's Method Number Three?" Colin inquired.

"Watch," said Drogel. He sat down on the carpeted

floor and flipped over onto his stomach. Then, with his hands holding the edge of the first step, he began lowering himself slowly. When he had gone as far as possible, he let go and dropped down to the second step. Snogel then sat down on the top step, pushed off, and landed neatly on Drogel's shoulders. "You're getting a touch heavy for this," Drogel groaned as he bent slightly at the knees to allow Snogel to hop off. The little men used this method for all fourteen steps.

"That really works up the appetite," said Snogel in the kitchen.

"I'm famished!" said Drogel.

Colin slid three slices of bread into the toaster (two for himself, and one for Snogel) and got a green apple out of the refrigerator for Drogel. He also brought out a peeler and a paring knife. He set these on the table beside the tall pilot.

"Are you sure you won't need any help with that?" Colin asked Drogel.

"Positive!" said Drogel.

The pilot grasped the peeler, one hand near each end, and circled the apple several times as if wondering how best to attack a dangerous animal. He then approached the round fruit and tried to peel a strip off it. But because he didn't have a free hand to hold the apple, it rolled away from him.

Snogel was watching from a distance, clearly enjoying his companion's predicament.

"Take that horrible grin off your face, Snogel, and come here," said Drogel. "I need your help."

"Will you help me with my toast?" Snogel asked slyly.

"Yes, yes," said Drogel impatiently. "Just come here and hold the silly apple still while I peel it."

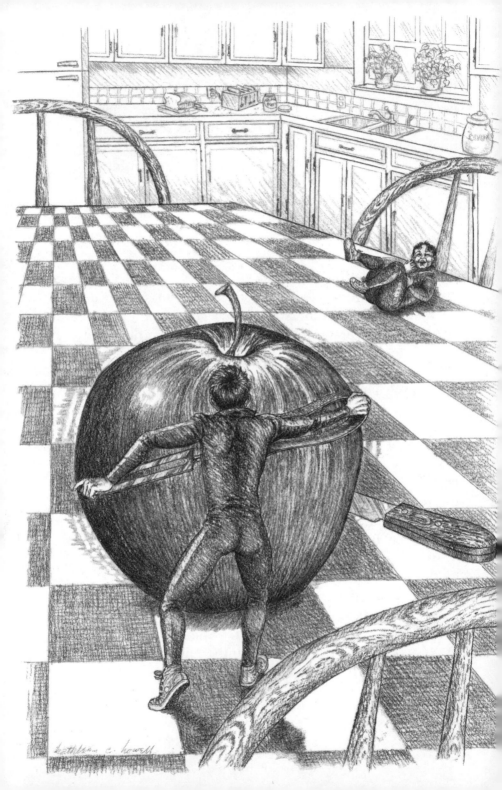

While Snogel braced the apple at the opposite side, Drogel peeled. It worked well. Halfway through the job, the toast popped up. It was golden brown.

"Is that dark enough for you, Snogel?" Colin asked.

"My goodness, no!" cried Snogel, looking over his shoulder. "Push it down for another go!"

Colin took out his two slices and put peanut butter on them.

Shortly after Drogel finished removing the green skin from the apple, Snogel's toast popped up again. It was becoming burnt around the edges.

"We're getting there," said Snogel. "Push the sucker down again, please, Colin."

"Stand clear, Snogel!" yelled Drogel. He was holding the paring knife above his head like a huge sword.

"Careful, Drogel!" cried Snogel, running to the other end of the table.

Just when it looked as if Drogel would topple over backward with the weight of the knife, he brought it down with such force that it cleaved the apple neatly in two.

"That was really something," said Colin, munching on his second piece of toast.

Smoke began spewing from the toaster.

Colin rushed over and popped up the black, hard toast. It was so hot he dropped it onto the counter. "Darn," he said. "It's completely ruined. I'll have to put another one in for you."

"Nonsense," said Snogel, looking at the smoking slice of bread. "It's perfect. It's exactly right."

Colin brought it over to Snogel on a plate. He also brought the jar of marmalade. Snogel didn't have much trouble buttering the toast, but he was not tall enough to put the knife into the marmalade jar.

"Drogel!" he called. "Your tallness is required."

By standing on his toes, Drogel was able to get a large gob of the orange stuff on the knife. He passed the knife to Snogel, who spread it on his toast.

Drogel sliced up the rest of his apple and began chomping away on it. Snogel was enjoying his toast immensely. They both ate with their gloves on.

Colin went to the refrigerator and poured himself a glass of milk.

"I'm thirsty, too," said Snogel, wiping marmalade off the side of his mouth with the sleeve of his space suit.

"What could you drink out of?" Colin said. "Glasses are much too big for you."

"Do you have any straws?"

"No," he said. "But you can use your helmet. I'll go upstairs and get it."

"Certainly not!" said Snogel. "That's outrageous!"

"Do you want a drink of milk or not?" Colin asked.

"Fine, fine."

"Could you bring me mine, too?" Drogel asked.

In less than a minute, Colin was back with the helmets. The pilots held them as Colin poured a small amount of milk into each.

"This is uncivilized and degrading," complained Snogel, but he raised the helmet to his mouth and took a drink.

"How did you eat and drink inside the game?" Colin asked when Snogel and Drogel had finished their meals.

"We had food lockers on the ship," said Snogel.

"Occasionally, at the delicatessen, we snuck out at night and helped ourselves to something or other. The salami Mr. Schmidt had there was quite good, wouldn't you say, Snogel?"

30

Snogel grunted in agreement.

Colin looked at the clock. It was a quarter to nine. "So," he said, "are you two ready to leave for Mr. Schmidt's?"

"Wash our helmets out well," said Snogel. "And dry them without getting fingerprints on them."

Colin rinsed the bubblelike helmets under the kitchen tap and dried them with a paper towel. Snogel and Drogel then fitted them carefully over their heads.

"This is really quite thrilling!" said Drogel.

"Be quiet, Drogel," muttered Snogel. "You aren't going to take us in that cramped pocket, are you, Colin?"

"I've got a jacket that has a larger pocket," Colin said. He ran back to his room and got it. "In you go," he said, placing the two pilots inside. The pocket bulged slightly, but Colin didn't think it was very noticeable. The same bulge could very well have been caused by a wallet. He wrote a note to his parents, telling them where he had gone, and then left the house.

Back to Meteoroids

When Colin, Snogel, and Drogel reached the delicatessen, Mr. Schmidt was sitting at a small table behind the counter, sorrowfully examining several bankbooks and a large pile of bills. He looked up as Colin walked in.

"Good morning, Mr. Schmidt," Colin said.

"I need money badly," Mr. Schmidt said in response. There was a small muscle twitching at the corner of his mouth. It made him look as if he were just on the verge of smiling. "The Meteoroids machine is fixed, Colin," he said quickly, his eyes narrowing. "I had a repairman come in late yesterday, and he had it working in a few minutes. Play as many games as you like."

An awful doubt seized Colin. If the game had been fixed, it meant there were two *other* little men in the spaceship!

"You *are* going to play, aren't you?" Mr. Schmidt asked hopefully. "I would really appreciate it if you played."

"Could you change a five-dollar bill for me?" Colin asked. *Would Snogel and Drogel be able to get inside the game?*

"I certainly could!" exclaimed Mr. Schmidt. He took Colin's bill and handed him twenty quarters.

"Thanks," said Colin. He walked to the Meteoroids game. There was nobody else in the shop. Mr. Schmidt was busy shuffling through slips of paper. Colin reached into his pocket and brought out Snogel and Drogel one at a time. He set them on the ledge of the machine.

"A repairman fixed the game," Colin whispered.

"We heard," Snogel said. He did not seem in the least concerned.

"But there are already pilots inside," Colin said. "Won't that be a problem?"

"Not at all," Drogel said. "Now, do you want us to enter and leave by the screen or by the back door?"

"Go in through the screen, but come out the back. That's safest, I think. Will there be any noise? When you two left the game yesterday, it flashed and groaned. There mustn't be any noise."

"And there won't be," promised Drogel. "Don't worry."

"Go ahead, then!"

"'Bye," said Snogel.

The two space pilots took a single long stride past the joystick and then jumped toward the television screen. Snogel was the first to hit—but *hit* is not the proper word, because he simply began disappearing into the screen. First his right arm and leg vanished, then his head and chest. . . .

And then . . .

And then . . .

He was gone!

Drogel slipped out of sight in the same way.

Then Colin saw—or thought he saw—the screen shimmer slightly, as water does when struck by a stone. But there was not a sound.

Colin glanced over his shoulder to make sure that Mr. Schmidt had not seen Snogel and Drogel's incredible entry. Mr. Schmidt had a hand over his face and was looking cautiously at a bankbook through two spread fingers.

After putting a quarter into the coin slot, Colin pressed the START button and waited. He placed his hands near the controls but did not touch them.

The small spaceship appeared on the screen, surrounded by six tumbling meteoroids. The ship remained motionless at first, but after a moment, it spun around fast and sped between two of the deadly outer-space rocks. Snogel and Drogel were in control! They had done it! Colin watched as the ship raced through space. He became entranced. It was almost as if he were in the ship with Snogel and Drogel. Never had the game been this exciting!

Occasionally someone entered the delicatessen to pick up a pound of hamburger or a bottle of salad dressing, but seldom did anyone travel far enough back in the shop to make Colin nervous. At one point, however, a teen-aged boy came in wanting to have a game of Meteor-oids. Colin grabbed hold of the joystick and tried his best to pretend he was actually playing. The teenager stood very close to him and watched the action taking place on the screen. Luckily for poor Colin, the boy lost patience after three or four minutes and left.

Two hours later, the spaceship had not even been bumped by a meteoroid.

"You've been playing an awfully long time," said Mr. Schmidt, walking toward Colin and rubbing his hands together hard. Colin clutched the joystick again and began pushing it about.

"How many games have you had?" Mr. Schmidt asked. "Ten? Fifteen? More than that?"

"I'm still on my first," Colin said.

"Oh," said the owner of the delicatessen. "I see." He turned and walked slowly away.

Half an hour passed. Snogel and Drogel were trapped in a dense meteoroid field. There was no escape. The two space pilots fought valiantly, but were finally crushed. The score flashing on the screen read:

11 285 810

Colin quickly went behind the game and waited. His eyes traveled over the back of the machine. He spotted a tiny, flickering black patch near the floor. And out of this patch came Snogel and Drogel. He saw the soles of their sneakers, then their legs, then the rest of their bodies.

"Yippeeeee!" cried Drogel.

"Far out!" bellowed Snogel.

Colin snatched them up and crammed them into his jacket pocket.

"What's all the noise about?" said Mr. Schmidt, approaching Colin. He then saw the score flashing in the upper right-hand corner of the video screen.

"Good heavens, boy!" he exclaimed, getting excited. "How did you get a score like that? Eleven million, two hundred and eighty-five thousand, eight hundred and ten! It must be the highest score anyone has ever made on this game! Are you going to enter the contest?"

"Which contest?" Colin asked quickly.

"The Meteoroids contest next Saturday. I have the advertisement taped up here somewhere. . . ." He walked over to the shop window and searched for a bit before ripping off a yellow sheet of paper. He handed it to Colin.

"Thank you very much," said Colin. "I'll think about this."

"You know, Colin," Mr. Schmidt began. "I don't suppose . . . I don't suppose . . ." He let his voice trail off again. "I don't suppose they allow betting at these sort of contests."

"I wouldn't think so, Mr. Schmidt," Colin told him. "Good-bye."

"That's too bad," Mr. Schmidt said quietly to himself.

Outside on the sidewalk, Colin looked at the advertisement.

This is what it said:

★ LOCAL METEOROIDS CHAMPIONSHIP ★
Ten o'clock Saturday morning, April 17
Crazy Rick's Amusement Center, 6521 Belmont Avenue

ATTENTION, ALL OUTSTANDING METEOROIDS PLAYERS!
IF YOU HAVE BEEN LOOKING FOR THE OPPORTUNITY
TO BECOME RICH AND FAMOUS, READ ON!

Grand Prize: $100 and a one-day free pass at Crazy Rick's.
Second Prize: $50 and a free haircut at the Mad Clipper's.
OTHER PRIZES TO BE WON!
ENTRANCE FEE: $2.50.

START PRACTICING! THE GRAND-PRIZE WINNER WILL GO ON
TO THE REGIONAL METEOROIDS CHAMPIONSHIP,
TAKING PLACE AT THE BEGINNING OF NEXT MONTH.

NOTE: ALL ENTRANTS MUST BE OVER TWO YEARS OF AGE.

Crazy Rick

37

At home, Colin found a note left for him by his mother. It was tacked to the bulletin board in the kitchen.

Colin, it read, *we've gone shopping and will be back shortly after one. If you get hungry, there are some roast beef sandwiches in the fridge. Love, Mom.*

In his bedroom, Colin lifted Snogel and Drogel out of his jacket pocket and set them on the night table. The pilots sat down on the handle of a hairbrush and removed their helmets.

"What was our score?" Drogel asked.

"It was over eleven million," Colin replied. "I can't remember the exact number."

"That isn't too bad for the first time," Snogel said. "When are we going in again? This afternoon? Tomorrow?" There was a sort of breathless expression on Snogel's face.

"I thought you said you weren't going to like doing this, Snogel," Colin said, smiling.

"That is correct," said Snogel slowly, looking down at his shoes. "I simply want to make sure that Drogel and I are prepared for any contest that comes our way. The money is what concerns me."

"He's lying," Drogel told Colin. "He liked flying the spaceship so much he didn't want to leave. I practically had to drag him out!"

Snogel turned red in the face. "Rubbish," he mumbled.

"Here, look at this," Colin said, placing the yellow advertisement in front of the tiny men. "What do you think, Drogel?"

"What do I think?" Drogel said, glancing over the piece of paper. "What do I think! We'll enter it, my dear boy. By all means, we'll enter it. This is incredibly lucky!"

"Nobody asked me what *I* think," Snogel said, folding his arms across his chest.

"What do you think, Snogel?" Drogel inquired politely.

"You don't really want my opinion," said Snogel.

"We do. We honestly do," said Drogel, nodding his head furiously.

"We simply cannot enter this contest."

"Why not?" Colin asked.

"Because it is being held at Crazy Rick's Amusement Center, that's why!" snapped Snogel. "I have no intention of returning to that place."

"You worked there?" Colin said.

"Before we were transferred to the deli," Drogel informed him.

"Crazy Rick is a madman," Snogel mumbled. "He's crackers. He's whacked right out. Once he nearly blew up the entire amusement center with dynamite. He said he loved the neat noise it made when exploding."

"He really wasn't *that* bad," Drogel said.

"How about Hack and Krack, then?" said Snogel. "They might be there again."

"Not a chance," said Drogel.

"Who are Hack and Krack?" Colin asked.

"You should tell him, Snogel," suggested Drogel.

"All right," the stout pilot said.

7

Galactic Gunmen

"Drogel and I used to pilot a Meteoroids ship at Crazy Rick's Amusement Center," Snogel began.

"There were two games at the center called Galactic Gunman, placed side by side against a wall. A hideous little man named Hack worked in one; a despicable person called Krack worked in the other. Both were obnoxious and vulgar, and neither of them ever took baths. Each carried a huge black rifle."

"They sound revolting," Colin said.

"After hours, when all the controllers were sitting on the ledges of their games, relaxing and talking to one another, Hack and Krack would scream insults at everyone—just sit there and call people names! Sometimes the two would have to think for several minutes to come up with a really rude name.

"One night, after the games room had been locked up, Hack and Krack remained silent for over two hours. Everyone else was sweating with fear, because whenever these two weren't busy name-calling, they were usually plotting away like mad, devising nasty plans.

"Then Hack said to his companion in a voice loud enough for all to hear, 'Heeeeey, Krack! How about a bit of *basketball* tonight?'

"Krack's blue face immediately broke into a disgusting thin-lipped smile. 'That sounds like a fine idea, Hack,' he said."

"What's so nasty about playing basketball?" Colin asked.

"Listen," Snogel said. "Both of the gunmen were looking straight at Sammy Sphere, who was unfortunate enough to be shaped like a rubber ball. He knew what Hack and Krack were thinking, and he started rolling toward the screen of his game. But he was not quick enough. The two gunmen jetted off their ledges, screeched across the room, and scooped him up.

"'We're having fun now!' said Krack, laughing horribly. The two men landed on the floor and started hurling Sammy about the room. They bounced him off the walls and ceiling. They rolled him like a bowling ball. This game lasted about fifteen minutes."

"Didn't you try to help Sammy?" Colin asked.

"Certainly I did!" cried Snogel. "We all did. But remember, my huge boy, that Hack and Krack had guns, and they were extremely foolhardy with these weapons. But later, when we were sure that the two gunmen were asleep in their games, we held a meeting with the rest of the controllers to decide what was to be done with the obnoxious couple. It was me, of course, who came up with the plan that solved our problems. Hack and Krack would never bother anyone again."

"It was actually my plan," Drogel whispered to Colin.

"Keep quiet, Drogel," growled Snogel. "I'm telling the story. Armed with a sprinkling of sugar, I crept into

Hack's game through the screen. *What* a horrid place it was! You could see nothing but desert wherever you looked. Hack was sleeping on a tall rock to avoid the Solar Slinkers. I—"

"The *what?*" cried Colin.

"The Solar Slinkers. They're wretched snaky things that shoot flaming streams of poison from their mouths. One drop of that stuff on your skin, and you're a goner!"

"Ugh," Colin said.

"I managed to speed across the sand without being attacked," Snogel went on. "I reached the snoring Hack. Beside him was his jet-pack. I unscrewed the cap to the fuel tank and poured my sugar inside."

"What does sugar do?" the youth asked.

"It burns out the valves, my boy. It completely clogs the engine!"

"Hooray!" Colin said.

"The following night, Hack and Krack were acting repulsive, as usual. They were picking their yellow teeth with broken-off toothpicks. Occasionally, one of them would let loose with a tremendous belch and then spit on the floor. It was thoroughly stomach-churning. Soon the insults began to flow from their foul mouths.

"They had just got warmed up when Sammy shouted, 'Oh, do *shut up,* you filthy slobs!' It was part of my plan. Hack and Krack were struck dumb. Nobody had ever called *them* names before.

"Hack was first to recover. 'Why, you cheeky brat!' he yelled. 'I think it's time for another round of basketball!' He switched on his jet-pack and flew off his game. He was halfway across the room when the sugar began to take effect."

Snogel was becoming really worked up now. The stout

pilot was pacing the night table and throwing his hands this way and that to emphasize his words.

"His jet-pack spluttered," Snogel said. "Then it wheezed. Then it coughed and smoked and died. Hack plummeted downward, a blank expression on his face. He landed with a mighty splash in a nearly full cup of Coke. It was beautiful. Everyone cheered."

"What happened to Krack?" Colin asked.

"Well," said Snogel, "after Hack had fallen into the soft drink, Krack flew up in the air and started shouting. The things he shouted were so rude that I couldn't possibly tell them to a young child like you. Now, Krack didn't know this, but up on the ceiling, far above him, was Milo. Milo was a controller for a game called Harpoon Hero, and he was armed with a suction-cup harpoon gun. Silo, his companion, was waiting on the floor. Just when Krack was about to take a shot at somebody, Milo fired his suction harpoon at Krack. It hit him square on the head and stuck. The gunman was so surprised that he dropped his rifle. 'I've been snagged!' he screamed. Milo fastened the end of the harpoon line around a light fixture. Then Silo fired his suction harpoon at Krack. It caught him on the seat of the pants. He tied his line to the leg of a chair. Krack was strung up in mid-air! He thrashed about violently, but was unable to free himself. He turned on his jet-pack but could not burn through the lines. Then he begged for mercy. It was quite a sight.

"'What shall we do with him?'" I shouted. Some told me to feed him to the Solar Slinkers. Others wanted to take off his clothes and burn them. But I had a better idea. With five other controllers, I climbed down to the floor. We grabbed hold of the line attached to Krack's

pants and pulled. We pulled until he was nearly touching the ground. The top wire was very taut. 'Now let go!' I cried. Krack rocketed back up and nearly got his head bashed on the ceiling. Then he fell down and bounced up again. We did this to him many times before we let him down. He was so dizzy he could barely stand. It was hilarious."

"What happened the next night?" Colin inquired.

"They left," said Drogel. "They packed up and left, they were so scared."

"I don't want to go back to Crazy Rick's," said Snogel quietly.

"Don't be childish, Snogel," scolded Drogel. "We're entering that contest."

Snogel said nothing. He was sulking.

"By the way, what did you do with the other two pilots in the spaceship today?" Colin asked. He sat down on the edge of his bed.

"Nothing much," said Drogel. "We asked them to get out of their seats and sit at the back of the ship. For some strange reason, Snogel insisted on tying their hands behind their backs and gagging them."

"It was loads of fun," Snogel said, forgetting he was supposed to be miserable. "That's the way all the secret agents do it."

"Actually," Drogel went on, "they would have been happy to see us if we hadn't landed right on top of them."

"Should have seen their faces," said Snogel. "They nearly passed away with fright."

"They were decent fellows," the tall pilot said. "Sog and Mog they were called. We untied them just before we left and shook hands so there wouldn't be any hard feelings between us."

"What was it like, flying the spaceship?" Colin wanted to know.

"It was marvelous," Drogel said.

"Nothing like it!" Snogel proclaimed.

"We were dodging those meteoroids and blasting away at everything in sight! You would like it, Colin. It's exhilarating!"

Colin smiled. "I think if we practice once a day until next Saturday, we'll walk away with the grand prize. To be honest, I don't think you two need any practice at all with the score you just got at Mr. Schmidt's."

"You're sure you don't want us to pilot again this afternoon?" Snogel asked.

"No, Snogel," said Colin, laughing.

"We need to change our plan," said Colin the day before the contest. "I won't be able to slip you two through the screen with all the people watching. You'll have to go in the back door, but I don't know how."

Colin, Snogel, and Drogel pondered this problem deeply for several minutes.

"Ah-ha!" cried Snogel triumphantly. "I have it. But please, let me think it out fully before I dazzle you with the absolute genius of it."

Drogel rolled his eyes and waited.

"What you must do, Colin, is set us down on the floor just before it is your turn to play. We will run across to the game and dive into it through the back way."

"You'll be spotted by the crowd," said Colin. "I can just see it now. The whole place would go wild."

"My poor misinformed boy," Snogel said. "We will not be seen. These shoes," he said, pointing to his sneakers, "allow us to move very quickly."

"Let me see you run," Colin said.

"He doesn't believe me," Snogel said to Drogel. "He simply does not believe that I can run so fast he won't be able to see me. Tell me when to start, Colin," he said, crouching over in a sprinter's starting position.

"On your mark, get set, go!"

Colin waited for the little man to bolt off in a blur. Snogel didn't move.

"I said go," Colin told Snogel.

"And I ran."

"I never saw you."

"I told you you wouldn't."

"Where did you go?" asked the youth.

"Across the blotting pad, past the telephone, around the lamp, and then back."

"That was fast," Colin said, amazed.

"I'm faster," Drogel said.

"Shut up, you fibber!" panted Snogel. "You're always saying that!"

"Then we're all set for the contest," Colin said. "Nobody can possibly see you enter the game. And remember to tie up the other pilots. I know it isn't a very nice thing to do, but if they decide to walk out while I'm pretending to play, it will ruin the whole thing."

"It isn't even going to be a contest," said Drogel confidently. "No one can compete with Snogel and me. We're the best!"

The Local Championship

"Name?" the man asked.

"Colin Filmore."

The man jotted this down on a paper-filled clipboard.

Crazy Rick's Amusement Center was crammed with teenagers. They were milling about, talking to one another in loud voices.

"Age?" the man asked, fairly shouting to be heard.

"Eleven."

"Great. Good luck to you, kid."

Colin paid his entrance fee and looked around the room. At the far end was a line of ten Meteoroids games.

There were many rows of chairs facing these games.

There was a long judges' table right up front.

Suddenly, out of the crowd, a man lunged toward Colin. He was wearing a red beanie with a small propeller on top. Two silver cap guns hung from a belt around his waist. He seized Colin's hand and began pumping it up and down furiously.

"What's your name, son?" he asked.

"Colin Filmore."

"I'm Rick, Crazy Rick, and I'm really thrilled to meet you!"

"I'm thrilled to meet you, too, sir," Colin said.

"I see that you're looking at my pistols," Rick said. "Do you like them? I haven't used them yet, and I'm just waiting for the chance. What a terrific noise they'll make! Oh, I see someone else coming inside. I must go and greet them. 'Bye, son."

He released Colin's hand and rushed away.

"You see!" Colin heard Snogel shout from his pocket. "He's going to shoot somebody with those guns! I just *knew* we shouldn't have come here!"

"Stop worrying, Snogel," said Drogel.

"It frightens me, Drogel. It really does. That man is extremely dangerous. Colin, were his weapons loaded?"

"They were only cap guns, Snogel," Colin said.

Drogel started laughing.

"Be quiet, Drogel!" Snogel screamed. "How was I to know they weren't real guns that sprayed out a bullet a second?"

Five minutes passed. Crazy Rick was standing on the judges' table, trying to get the attention of the crowd.

"Please take your seats," he said.

Nobody heard him.

"Please!" he shrieked. "Please, will you all sit down and stop talking!"

Everyone stopped and looked up at Rick for a moment, decided he was out of his mind, and then continued their deafening conversations.

Crazy Rick took his two cap guns out of their holsters and fired them at the ceiling.

The crowd fell silent.

"Now sit down," he said.

Everyone sat down.

"Thank you. Now, if you will listen to Bud for a couple of seconds, we can start the contest. Bud, come up here."

The man who had signed Colin in clambered onto the table and stood beside Rick. He took a pair of dark sunglasses from his pocket and put them on.

"Okay. You will be called up in groups of ten to take your turns. You will also be assigned a number that tells you what game to go to. The game on the far left is number one, the one beside it is number two, and so on. There will be a ten-minute play limit. Your turn ends when ten minutes is over or when your spaceship is destroyed, whichever comes first. Your goal is to score as many points as possible. No questions? Fantastic!"

"Is that all you have to say, Bud?" Crazy Rick asked.

"That's it, Rick."

"Then let the contest begin!" cried Rick, jumping off the table and twirling the propeller on his beanie.

"Only ten minutes to play, you two," Colin said quietly, tapping his pocket.

"Yes, yes," came Snogel's voice. "We're not deaf!"

The first set of competitors was already beginning. One teenager did not last the ten minutes. As he walked dejectedly back to his chair, Crazy Rick called out his score for all to hear.

"Twenty-five thousand, seven hundred and thirty. That is disgusting! My goldfish has done better than that!"

As the contest progressed, Colin began to feel nervous. He wondered if Snogel and Drogel could work well in such a short space of time. When they had piloted the ship at the delicatessen, they had had as much time as they wanted.

50

The highest score so far was 210,580.

". . . five, Harry Walker," Bud was shouting. "Six, Martin Warburg; seven, Colin Filmore . . ."

"Now!" Colin heard a muffled voice exclaim. He reached into his pocket and grabbed the two space pilots and lowered them to the floor. No sooner had their sneakers hit the carpet when they were gone, running at an incredible speed toward game number seven.

Colin stood up and walked over to the games with nine other competitors. They took their places by the controls. They waited.

"On your marks, get set, go!" cried Crazy Rick.

Ten START buttons were pressed down at the same moment. Colin grasped his joystick with one hand and, with the other, pressed buttons. It was easy to pretend he was playing, with no one watching closely. Snogel and Drogel's ship was a blur on the screen. Diving. Climbing. Swerving to the right. Swerving to the left. Firing.

"Stop!" yelled Rick, ten minutes later.

Colin released the joystick and went back to his seat. Crazy Rick and Bud rushed up to the games and copied down the scores.

"Seven hundred and fifty thousand, three hundred and eighty!" gurgled Rick, banging a clipboard against his forehead to make sure he was seeing properly. "That was on number seven. Who was on number seven?"

"Seven . . . seven," mumbled Bud, running a finger down a column of names. "Colin Filmore! Yes, Colin Filmore on number seven!"

Some people in the audience booed. Most clapped and cheered.

At his chair, Colin bent over and fidgeted with his

shoelaces. And then, out of nowhere, Snogel and Drogel were standing beside his hand, smiling behind their helmets. Colin quickly put the two pilots back into his pocket. He glanced at the teenagers sitting next to him. They were both watching the following group of competitors.

Near noon, everybody had taken their turns. It took Rick and Bud only a second to determine the grand-prize winner: Colin Filmore. Crazy Rick asked him up to the judges' table, where he was congratulated.

"That was quite a show, son. I take my hat off to you." He lifted the beanie off his head. "Here's your check for one hundred dollars as well as a free pass at my place for a whole day. Also, you have earned the honor of being eligible to compete in the Regional Meteoroids Championship." For emphasis, he fired off his cap guns several times.

Colin left the amusement center immediately.

Outside on the sidewalk, he heard Snogel say, "We are on our way!"

The Wait

"Doubles!" cried Drogel. "Two fours!"

Colin, Snogel, and Drogel were playing a game of Monopoly the Monday after the Meteoroids contest. Colin had just come home from school, and his parents were still at work. He was using a red plastic shoe as his marker. Snogel and Drogel were using themselves.

"Phew!" panted Drogel after jogging down the length of the board. "That was a long way to go. I'm on Boardwalk. Does anybody own it?"

"Hurry up and go again!" snapped Snogel. "You have to go again if you roll doubles."

"Not so quickly, my impatient friend," said Drogel. "If nobody owns Boardwalk, I'll buy it. Ah-ha! Now I have the set!"

"Hand over the money first," grumbled Snogel, who was acting as the banker. "Do you have enough money?"

"Of course I do!" exclaimed Drogel, walking over to a wad of five-hundred-dollar bills. He paid for the property and took the title-deed card. "Now I get to go again."

54

Drogel lifted the dice one at a time and threw them down on the center of the board. "Seven," he said, walking leisurely. "I passed Go. That'll be two hundred, Snogel. . . . And here I am on another unbought lot. I'll take this one, too."

Snogel groaned. "I'm sure you have the dice weighted, Drogel. You're snapping up all the choice lots."

"Simply luck," Drogel said. "There we are. It's your turn now, Colin."

Colin took the dice and rolled. "What are you planning to do with your share of the prize money?"

"What are you going to do with yours?" Snogel asked.

"Put it in my bank account."

"We'll put ours in your bank account, too. That way, it accumulates in value, and your parents won't ask where the rest of your hundred dollars went."

"Good idea," Colin said, moving his little shoe. "What will you do when you've won a lot of prize money?"

"We will definitely travel to Hawaii," Drogel said.

"No," Snogel corrected. "Florida."

"Terribly sorry, Snogel," said Drogel, "but Hawaii is a much nicer spot than Florida."

"I want to see Disney World."

"Don't be difficult."

"It's your turn, Snogel," said Colin, wanting to avoid a tense scene.

"Where is the Regional Championship?" Drogel asked.

"It's being hosted by Crazy Rick's," Colin replied.

"You mean we have to go there again?" Snogel said. Colin nodded.

"He'll have real guns this time," Snogel mumbled, shaking his head.

"I think this next contest is going to be quite a bit

harder than the last one," said Colin. "Kids from all over will be there."

"Don't worry," Drogel told him. "It'll be a snap. We get better every time we play."

"It's the waiting that bothers me," Colin said. "I just wish the competition were tomorrow so that we could get it over with. Every day I become more and more excited. It's got so that I have trouble concentrating in school."

"Relax," said Snogel. "You are much too nervous."

"I'm going to put up hotels!" Drogel declared suddenly.

"You have to wait until your turn!" said Snogel.

"It *is* my turn, you silly beast! Here are four five-hundred-dollar bills. Keep the change and hand over two red hotels. Aren't they beautiful, Colin? Just look at them."

"They're hideous," said Snogel.

"How often do you two want to practice?" Colin asked.

"Once a day, as usual," said Snogel.

"What we should do," suggested Drogel, "is practice playing for fifteen- or twenty-minute periods to see how many points we can possibly earn in so little time. There's bound to be a time limit at this next competition, too."

"That's a super idea, Drogel," Colin said. "We'll do that. We can go to Crazy Rick's and play for a whole day on our free pass."

"A whole day with Crazy Rick!" Snogel muttered.

Colin took his turn at Monopoly.

Snogel was next. He threw the dice and started walking. He stopped on Boardwalk.

"It's your turn, Drogel," he said quickly.

"You have landed smack on my giant hotel!" Drogel cried. "That'll be two thousand bucks!"

"It isn't fair!" yelled Snogel. "It just isn't fair!" He looked at Drogel. He looked up at Colin and smiled wickedly. He then ran toward the red hotel and kicked it off the board.

"Let's call it a game," Colin said. "You two can clean up." He went downstairs and picked up the newspaper on the doorstep before sitting down in the living room. He took out the Entertainment section, and as he was flipping through the pages to the comics, he came across a large picture of himself. He was shaking hands with Crazy Rick and holding the envelope that contained the check and free pass. Colin read what was written below the photo:

Eleven-year-old Colin Filmore won the Local Meteoroids Championship Saturday at Crazy Rick's Amusement Center. Colin competed against people up to nineteen years of age and went away with the grand prize of one hundred dollars and a free pass for a day at the amusement center. Colin's score was over three-quarters of a million points—an incredible accomplishment, as there was a ten-minute play limit. Colin is expected to compete in the regional contest on the first of next month.

Colin ran back upstairs and showed the picture to Snogel and Drogel.

"You're famous," Drogel said.

"I didn't get *my* picture in the paper," Snogel mumbled. "I did much more work than Colin!"

"My horrible friend," said Drogel. "Without Colin's brilliant idea, none of this would be happening. You should consider yourself lucky to take part in such a fantastic adventure."

"I hope I end up filthy rich at the end of this fantastic adventure," Snogel muttered.

"Oh, do stop being so greedy!" exclaimed the tall pilot. "I've never known anyone more selfish than you."

"Hurry up and put your Monopoly money away," Snogel said.

"I haven't finished counting it yet," said Drogel primly. "It's important to me to know how much I had."

"Now look who's the money-minded one," Snogel whispered to Colin as Drogel walked carefully among his stacks of bills.

"Four thousand, two hundred and five," Drogel counted, "four thousand, two hundred and fifty five . . ."

"You know, Colin," Snogel observed, "I wouldn't be at all surprised if after this next contest, your face was plastered on billboards."

Colin raised his eyebrows and tried to picture this.

"Five thousand, twenty-six dollars!" Drogel cried.

"I just wish that I didn't have to go into Crazy Rick's place again," Snogel said, ignoring his ecstatic friend.

"After the Regional Championship, probably you will never have to," Colin told him.

"Good," said Snogel.

"What are you going to do with the hundred dollars you won at the contest?" Colin's father asked that night at the dinner table.

"Put it in my bank account," said Colin.

"You know what, Colin?" his father said in a hushed voice. "You know what?"

"What, Dad?" Colin asked.

"I think you should invest in stocks!" Mr. Filmore was

getting very excited, and he began winding the corkscrew into the table.

"Darling!" cried Mrs. Filmore. "You're drilling a hole in our mahogany table!"

"Oh. Sorry about that, dear. Anyway, Colin, I know a stockbroker who would invest that prize money for you."

"It's only a hundred dollars, Dad. I don't think it's enough. I'll just put it in the bank."

"All right," said Mr. Filmore, looking somewhat put out. "It's your money. I was just trying to help you."

"Maybe if I win the next competition," Colin said, "I'll have enough to invest."

"I didn't know you were so good at Meteoroids," Colin's mother admitted. "Just make sure that this next contest doesn't start interfering with your schoolwork."

"I will," Colin assured her.

"When is it, this Regional Championship?" his father asked, pouring himself a glass of red wine.

"The first of May," Colin replied, feeling excited just mentioning the date.

The Regional Championship

"Great to see you again, kid!" Crazy Rick hollered, grabbing Colin by the shoulders and shaking him rapidly back and forth. "Did you get a good night's rest? Oh . . . oh, do I see bags under your eyes, son? I certainly hope not. Well, blow 'em away again, son. I have absolute faith in you."

Every time Rick shook Colin, Snogel and Drogel were jostled about in his jacket pocket.

"He always was very strange, the way he greeted people," Drogel said as he bumped into Snogel's helmeted head.

"The man's completely crackers!" Snogel snarled. "I wish I had a stun gun!"

Once again, the amusement center was crammed, not so much with contestants this time as with reporters and photographers. The reporters were holding their little notepads and tape recorders, and the photographers were examining the flashes on their cameras.

"All right!" yelled Bud. "If you will all sit down, we can get this thing under way. People from the press, will you please sit at the tables along the sides? Super. Now, I know I speak for Rick when I say that we're happy to host this prestigious competition."

There was a long round of applause.

"The time limit," Bud continued, "has been set at twenty minutes, as there are only forty people competing today. And one last item: Rick and I have just learned that the National Meteoroids Championship will be held in San Francisco at the end of this month. All of you here have the chance to qualify for it. To do this, you must not only win the contest, you must win with a score of *at least* three hundred and twenty thousand!"

"That's impossible!" Colin heard the teenager beside him gasp.

The contest was identical to the last one. Long rows of chairs were arranged in front of the line of ten Meteoroids games. The contestants were called up in groups of ten to take their turns, and afterward the scores were shouted out. Occasionally, the click of a camera could be heard.

Colin was in the last set of competitors. As his name was called, he placed Snogel and Drogel on the floor, and they sped off into the proper game.

Crazy Rick fired his cap gun once. Colin hit his START button. Snogel and Drogel began slowly, earning only fifteen thousand points in thirty seconds (Snogel later blamed it on Drogel's clumsy steering). But by the end of twenty minutes, the score on the screen flashed:

1 602 750

Crazy Rick was so impressed he was pulling his hair out in large tufts. He danced from table to table, bellowing to all the reporters that he had known Colin since he was three years old and that he himself had trained the boy to play Meteoroids.

There were reporters from the two local papers and from all the surrounding cities and districts. There was even a slick-looking newsman from a famous national magazine who wore mirrored sunglasses and had a cigarette dangling from a corner of his mouth. In all, they were a pretty uptight lot. They were clambering over one another, trying desperately to reach the young winner. None of them were listening to Crazy Rick.

"What school do you attend?" one reporter asked Colin. "Where do you live?" another wanted to know. "How old are you?" "How long have you been playing this game?" "Do you have a system worked out?" "Have you practiced a lot for this competition?" "What are your ambitions in life?" "What brand of shoes do you wear?" "Do you have a dog?"

At first, Colin was rather enjoying all the attention he was receiving. But when the cameras kept flashing and the newsmen continued asking questions and shoving microphones in his face, he began to get annoyed and tired. The reporters, however, did not seem to notice this, or if they did, they didn't care one little bit.

Colin was soon saved by Crazy Rick. Rick, obviously flustered at having been left out, went to the back of the amusement center and triggered the fire alarm. This produced enough noise and consternation within the building to scatter the crowd of reporters around Colin long enough for Rick to reach him.

"I would just like to say that this here eleven-year-old boy is truly amazing. You can quote me on that one," Rick told a reporter. "He definitely has a valuable skill that I helped develop."

Rick handed a large white envelope to Colin. Inside

was a check for a thousand dollars and an entry form for the National Meteoroids Championship.

"This kid's the best!" Rick shouted. "He can't answer any more questions, though. You can ask *me* questions, but not the boy. He's bushed. He needs his rest if he's going to be ready for the National. Make way for the boy!" Rick whipped out one of his cap guns and fired a couple of warning shots over a terrified reporter's head. "Move aside there!"

When Colin was nearly at the exit, he suddenly remembered that he had not picked up Snogel and Drogel. He glanced around quickly and saw them standing between a reporter's legs, waving their arms at him. Colin dropped the white envelope with the prize money, and as he stooped to retrieve it, he scooped up the two tiny men and shoved them into his pocket. Then he was outside on the street corner, away from the din of the amusement center. He began walking home.

"Wow!" said Snogel from the pocket. "I was scared we were going to be left behind in there! That was very close."

Fame and Math Homework

"A thousand dollars!" exclaimed Snogel happily.

"National coverage," gasped Drogel.

All three adventurers were looking over the check and the latest edition of a well-known magazine. The cover of the magazine showed Colin standing in front of Meteoroids at the last contest, and inside there was a lengthy article about Colin and video games in general. The article began with the word *Unreal!*

The local newspapers had already printed another photo of Colin, along with small write-ups about him and the prizes he had won and was expected to win.

"When I first came up with my idea," said Colin, "I never thought it would result in something like this."

"Well, you're famous now, Colin," Snogel told the boy. "You may as well enjoy it."

"And it isn't going to end here," Drogel said. "After we win this nationwide contest, your name, my dear boy, will be known in every household across the country!"

"I think it's getting out of hand," Colin said with a chuckle. "In the past few days, I have received phone calls from people who just wanted to hear my voice. I have also received piles and piles of fan mail from people—mostly kids my own age—who all want me to write back to them! At school, a lot of people hang around me and ask questions about Meteoroids, like how I got so good at the game. Yesterday I had a close call. Some teenagers wanted to see me play the game at lunchtime. They even offered to pay for it. Luckily, I had a detention then for not doing my homework."

"Hold it!" growled Drogel. "You haven't been doing your homework? Have you worked on the assignments that are due tomorrow?"

Colin looked away from the little man. "No."

"Why not?" demanded Snogel.

"Well, I've been thinking a lot about the contest that is coming up, and I really haven't been concentrating in class, so when the teacher assigns homework, I don't know how to do it."

"Hmm. You should have gone to your teachers for help, but Snogel and I will see what we can do. What's first?"

"Math. It's pretty hard stuff, though. Mr. Talbot has come back from the hospital—remember I told you how he knocked himself out—and he's giving us these word problems that I honestly don't think have answers."

"Child's play," said Snogel. "Let's see."

Colin flipped open his exercise book to the proper page. "Here it is."

Drogel walked onto the page and read the question aloud.

"'Mr. Jenkins has three sons. His first son plays the violin. His second son likes to eat carrot cake, and his youngest son is five years old. If the house in which Mr. Jenkins lives has eight windows, how old are his other two children? Show workings clearly. No guessing!'"

Drogel read the question over once more.

"Well," he said, "it's simple. You must divide by ten."

"Divide *what* by ten?" Colin asked.

"The number of windows," Drogel stammered.

"No, no, you clod!" yelled Snogel, pushing Drogel out of the way. "That is not the way it is done! It is actually very easy. We are already told that one child is five, are we not?"

Colin nodded. "But how, Snogel, does that help us?"

"It doesn't," Snogel replied. "I'm just working myself up. Now then, we know that one child likes to eat carrot cake. He is obviously seven."

"Why?" Colin asked.

"Because all seven-year-olds like to eat carrot cake!" said Snogel, exasperated. "Now, the fact that the oldest child plays the violin must be a clue of some sort. How many notes can one play on a violin, Colin?"

"I don't know."

"Neither do I," admitted Snogel. "So we'll just say that the oldest boy is eleven."

"Sounds good to me," Colin said, copying numbers into his notebook.

"So, what's next?" asked Drogel.

"English."

"No problem," Snogel said.

"All right. Who wrote *Romeo and Juliet*?" Colin wanted to know.

"Alfred Hitchcock!" cried the stout pilot.

"Oh, you do make me a bit ill, Snogel," Drogel said. "Alfred Hitchcock certainly did not write *Romeo and Juliet*. Bill Shortspeare wrote it. It's a very famous play."

"Bill Shortspeare, that's right," Snogel agreed. "I've heard the name before."

"You two are really pretty smart," Colin said.

"We *are* space pilots," Drogel pointed out.

"You have to be smart to pilot a spaceship," Snogel added.

"Just one more thing," said Colin. "Geography. We have to name all ten Canadian provinces from west to east."

"Hmmmmm," said Drogel.

"Ahhhhh," said Snogel.

"I'll start you off. British Columbia."

"Alberta!" Snogel shouted.

"What next?" prodded Colin.

"Sasquatchewan!" Drogel yelled.

"Close enough. What then?"

"Womanitoba?" asked Snogel.

"*Manitoba!*" corrected Drogel. "Not *Womanitoba!*"

"Ontario."

"Oh . . . ah . . . Quebec!"

"Good. What else?" Colin said.

"Nothing else," stated Drogel.

"What do you mean, *nothing else?*" Colin demanded.

"I mean that there are no more provinces after Quebec. It's the last one. No more."

"There are ten provinces! You have named only six."

"I have to agree with Drogel," Snogel said.

"You two are impossible!" Colin exclaimed. "You are telling me that there are only six provinces in Canada?"

"Yes."

"Exactly."

"Well," said Colin, looking through his atlas, "it says here that there are ten—let's see . . . New Brunswick, Nova Scotia, Prince Edward Island, and Newfoundland."

"Have you heard of those?" Drogel whispered to Snogel. "I sure haven't."

"I haven't either," Snogel whispered back. "I think he's gone funny in the head."

Drogel said, "It's all the excitement."

Then the two space pilots erupted with laughter. They rolled on the desktop, holding their sides. Tears were streaming out of their eyes.

"You . . . should have . . . seen . . . your . . . face," Snogel managed to say.

"We really had . . . you . . . there!" Drogel said, giggling.

"It's okay. I can take a joke," Colin said, smiling sweetly. "Oh!" he added suddenly. "Did I tell you there will be no supper tonight? I didn't? Well, there won't be. My father's law firm has gone bankrupt, and my mother was fired. No money to buy groceries. Sorry about that."

Drogel and Snogel quickly stopped laughing.

"You *are* joking, aren't you?" asked Drogel.

"He's joking," Snogel said. There were vertical worry lines appearing in his forehead.

"Sure I'm joking," Colin told them, keeping a stony face.

"This isn't funny, Colin," Snogel croaked. "We could starve. And where would that get you? You wouldn't be able to win the National Championship."

It was now Colin's turn to laugh.

"Never do that again," said Drogel, breaking into a wide grin.

"That's a lot of money, a thousand dollars, Colin," his father said at suppertime. "I think you could invest in a really super-duper stock."

70

"Leave the boy alone, dear," Mrs. Filmore reprimanded. "And stop pouring salad dressing into your wineglass!"

"Terribly sorry, my sweet," Mr. Filmore said.

"Investing is too risky, Dad," Colin pointed out. "Look what happened to Mr. Schmidt."

"What happened?" Colin's mother asked.

"He lost so much money investing that he went out of business."

"He was a gambling man, though," Mr. Filmore said. "He probably lost all his money playing poker."

"I'll just put the money in my account for the time being."

"Sure. Fine." Mr. Filmore sighed.

Colin's mother asked, "Do you really want to go to this national competition in San Francisco, Colin?"

Colin looked up at his parents. "Yes, I do want to go. I want to go very much."

"We just didn't want you to go because you felt you had to, that's all," explained his father, smiling warmly. "But if you want to go, that's all right with us. It *is* paid for by the contest sponsors, isn't it?"

"Yes, Dad."

"Great. Keeping up with your schoolwork?"

"Yes, I—" Colin was about to say that he was helped by Snogel and Drogel, but he caught himself in time. "Yes, I'm keeping up with all my work."

"I'm proud of you, son. Keep it up."

"I will, Dad. Pass the milk, please."

The day of the big contest neared.

Pictures of Colin continued to appear in various newspapers and magazines, and Colin continued to receive phone calls and letters from his admirers. He tried

to write back to as many of these people as possible, but it proved such a big task that he was forced to make up a form letter. It looked something like this:

Dear _____,

Thank you so very much for your letter/phone call. I am fine. How are you? The weather here today is sunny/rainy/windy/all three. At school I do such interesting things as: _____. I will be competing in the National Meteoroids Championship soon, and I hope to win it. My hobbies are playing Meteoroids (of course), reading, swimming, and skydiving (a very tricky sport). What are your hobbies? I live in a nice house. My father is a lawyer, and my mother is a real-estate agent. I will probably become a professional Meteoroids player when I grow up. Thanks again for your letter.

Best regards,

Colin Filmore

"Perfect," said Snogel.

"It makes you sound very professional," Drogel commented, "especially the part about your skydiving."

"I've never skydived in my life," Colin said.

"That's not the point," declared Snogel. "The more professional you appear, the bigger appeal you have with the public."

"Really?" said Colin.

"Yes."

"Snogel," demanded Drogel, "where did you ever learn something like that?"

"At college."

"You never told me you went to college!"

"It was a very long time ago," Snogel said.

The Flight

It was the day before the big contest in San Francisco. At nine in the morning, Colin, Snogel, and Drogel boarded a long, wide-bodied jet at the airport. It was the first time Colin had ever been inside an airplane, and a pretty blonde stewardess led him down an aisle to his window seat. The man sitting beside him was listening to a pair of headphones that plugged into the arm of his chair.

"Are we in the air yet?" squeaked Snogel from Colin's pocket.

"We just walked on board, how could we have taken off already?" Colin replied quietly.

"Just tell me when we're in the air, then."

"You aren't nervous about flying, are you, Snogel?" Colin asked.

"You bet your trousers I'm nervous!" Snogel snapped. "I'm as nervous as a cat on a hot tin roof!"

"Didn't you used to work in London?"

"Yes."

"Well, then," said Colin, "you must have flown in a jet to get across the Atlantic Ocean."

"Ah. We took a cruise ship, you see," Snogel explained.

Drogel was much more relaxed about the situation than Snogel.

"Wonderful machines, these jets, wouldn't you say so, Colin?"

"Yes, they're marvelous."

"Do you know how one flies?"

"No. I haven't the slightest idea."

"Well, I'll tell you, then. Underneath the wings of the plane are hundreds—no, thousands of birds. When those birds flap their wings, they make the plane lift off the ground. The pilots of the plane send instructions to the birds through an intercom. The birds do whatever the pilots say. Being an airline pilot is a very cushy job, let me tell you. They sit around and eat cookies all day long in the cockpit."

"Oh, oh, *oh!*" moaned Snogel. "How on earth can you fib to the boy like that, Drogel? That is not the way a plane flies. Everyone in his right mind knows that a plane can fly because it is strung on hooks and runs on a track through the sky."

"And what holds the track in the sky, if I may be so bold as to ask?" questioned Drogel.

"It is, as yet, a mystery," mumbled Snogel. "Colin, have we taken off yet?"

"Yes, we took off ten minutes ago."

"I think I'm going to be ill."

"Snogel, get a grip on yourself!" shouted Drogel. "You are not going to be ill. Now just calm down."

"I'm going to be ill, I just know it," said Snogel.

"Shut up! You will make yourself ill if you keep on dancing about like that. Now sit down and read your book."

Book? Colin thought.

Half an hour passed peacefully. Breakfast was served, and Colin slipped the two pilots part of a roll and a strip of bacon.

"You know what, Colin?" Drogel said suddenly.

"What?"

"I'd like to fly this jet. I would very much like to sit in the enormous cockpit and give orders to all those birds under the wings."

"Don't let him!" shrieked Snogel in terror.

"I don't think right now is the best time, Drogel," Colin said. "The last thing we want is for you to be seen."

"Oh, all right." Drogel sighed.

"I have been badly scared," Snogel said in a quavering voice. "I have to go to the washroom."

"Do you really?" demanded Drogel.

"Yes."

"It's at the back of the airplane. You'll have to rush down the aisle," instructed Drogel. "Be careful you don't get stepped on. Remember how devastating it was last time you were trodden on. Try to crawl under the door, or if that doesn't work, push the door slightly ajar and slip in. But make sure that the washroom is not being used by somebody else. The sign on the door should say VACANT."

"Could you let me down to the floor?" Snogel asked Colin, poking his head out of the pocket.

Colin removed the stout pilot from the pocket and placed him on the floor when he was certain that the man beside him (who was *still* listening to the arm of his seat) wasn't looking.

"Remember where you're sitting," Colin warned. And with that, Snogel sped off toward the rear of the plane.

Shortly after Snogel returned, feeling much better, a stewardess came around.

"Would you like a pair of headphones for the movie?" she asked Colin. "You just plug them in here," she said, pointing to the arm of his chair.

"Thanks," said Colin.

The in-flight movie was called *The Invasion of the Ant People*. By sitting on Colin's shoulder closest to the window, out of sight, Snogel and Drogel could not only watch the film, they could hear the sounds from Colin's headphones. They were horrible squelching and screeching noises.

Drogel watched with fascination. Snogel had to make three more trips to the washroom.

Lunch was served after the movie ended.

It was close to noon (San Francisco time, of course) when the jet made a smooth landing at the San Francisco International Airport. And it was here that Colin Filmore got a rather nasty shock. His parents had arranged that someone involved with the Meteoroids contest would meet him at the airport and take him to his hotel. No sooner had Colin walked off the plane and started down a long corridor when he saw, standing against a wall, a very familiar person: Crazy Rick!

Sneaking Out

"Thought I gave up on you, huh, kid?" said Crazy Rick, twirling the propeller on his beanie. "I was allowed to come because I said I was your trainer. I was on the very same flight as you. I guess you never noticed me. Wasn't that ant movie super? I was cheering for those invaders all the way!"

"Hang on!" snapped Snogel from inside Colin's jacket pocket. "Whose voice was that? It sounded a tad like Crazy Rick's."

"That's because it was Crazy Rick's," Drogel replied, wiping at a small stain on his space suit.

Colin heard a groan of utter despair come from his pocket.

"What was that groaning noise I heard, son? Have you had any breakfast?" Colin nodded. "How about lunch?"

"I had lunch as well," Colin told him.

"Where have you been eating all these meals, son?" Rick asked, incredulous.

"On the airplane, of course," said Colin.

"Isn't that something," said Rick, shaking his head. "I guess I was ripped off. I saw the person next to me eating off a tray in front of him, but I thought he had brought his own food! That really is something!"

With that, Rick led Colin out of the airport and looked up and down the road for a taxi. There wasn't one in sight. Then he saw a young man in a greenish uniform standing at the curb. Rick walked up to him.

"Where do I get a taxi?" Rick asked, fingering the cap guns around his waist.

"Right here," the porter said, handing Rick a small ticket with the number *115* written on it.

"What the heck's this?" Rick cried. "I want a taxi, not a piece of paper."

"You must wait your turn like everyone else," the uniformed man told Rick, pointing toward a group of people holding suitcases.

A cab pulled up along the curb in front of the porter. "Number 112!" he yelled. A lady waved her ticket in the air, and the uniformed man walked over to her and grabbed her bags, carrying them to the waiting taxi. The lady handed him a five-dollar bill before getting inside.

"Did you see that?" Rick exclaimed, tapping Colin on the shoulder. "You've got to pay even to get into a taxi!"

"Number 113!

"Number 114!

"Number 115!"

"Right over here!" Rick bellowed. The porter winced slightly and sauntered toward Rick.

"Any luggage?" he inquired.

"Just what we're carrying," Colin said.

"This way, then."

The porter led them to a taxi, opened the door, and watched them climb in. Then he waited. His right hand was twitching in the anticipation of a tip.

"Watch this," Rick whispered to Colin. He reached into

his pocket and brought out a light blue, fifty-dollar bill. It was Monopoly money. Rick pressed this into the porter's hand.

The porter's eyes flicked down onto the bill for a split second, seeing only the number 50 printed large.

"Thank you, sir!" the porter burbled. "Oh, hold on a second, sir, I see a little speck of dust on your pant leg. Here, please let me brush it off. Thank you very much, sir. I hope to see you again sometime." He closed the car door and skipped away.

"Poor sucker," Rick said, grinning horribly.

"Where to?" the cab driver asked.

"The Royal York."

The automobile screamed away from the curb. Shortly it was driving along a busy highway. On either side were high-rise apartments and an occasional small factory. Within twenty minutes, the taxi had stopped in front of a large hotel.

"Twenty-three dollars," the cab driver said.

Rick paid him.

A porter rushed over to the cab and opened the door.

"No luggage? Follow me, please, gentlemen."

He led them into an enormous lobby and directed them to the reception desk. This man expected no tip.

Colin and Rick were in separate rooms right across from one another. Rick signed in at the desk and took the door keys. The two rode up to their floor in the elevator.

"Now, I want you to stay in your room and rest up," said Rick as they walked down the hallway. "You'll need all your strength for the contest tomorrow morning. At six thirty this evening, I'll knock on your door, and we'll go down and have supper in the dining room. I'm starved, you know. I haven't eaten all day!"

Rick gave Colin his key, and they entered their rooms.

Colin locked the door and turned on the lights. He removed Snogel and Drogel from his pocket and set them on one of the double beds. The room was large, with a bathroom and sitting room included. At one end of the room, a set of glass doors led onto a small balcony overlooking downtown San Francisco.

"What luxury!" exclaimed Drogel.

"Posh," Snogel said.

Colin flopped onto the other double bed. "What shall we do until supper? Watch TV?"

"Certainly not!" cried Drogel. "We are going to take in the sights of San Francisco!"

"You're mad!" Snogel said.

"Why do you say that?" Drogel asked.

"Because this is a large city, and it is not safe to walk the streets in a big city. Just think for a moment, if you will, of the crime and corruption."

"Snogel," Drogel began slowly, "it's the middle of the afternoon. Nothing can possibly happen to us. It isn't as if we were going out at two in the morning!"

"Oh," said Snogel.

"I don't know," Colin said. "Crazy Rick might be sitting in the lobby, just waiting for me to come out. He'll make me go back to my room. And who knows what might happen if he gets excited. He could make an incredible scene."

"He could shoot us," said Snogel.

"Forget Crazy Rick," Drogel ordered. "It's a simple matter of logic. If Crazy Rick is waiting for us anywhere, he will obviously be at the elevator, because he, not being as clever as me, will think that we would take that route to the lobby. We will take the stairs down."

"Brilliant," Snogel said.

"Do you think it will work?" Colin asked.

"Can't fail!" Drogel declared.

"Let's try it," Colin said, beginning to feel excited.

"Wait a second!" said Drogel as Colin was about to put him and Snogel into the jacket pocket. "How are we supposed to see the sights in there?"

"I should poke a couple of holes through the fabric, but I don't have a pair of scissors or anything sharp."

"Try this," said Snogel, holding out a tiny jackknife that he had taken from a pocket somewhere in his trousers.

The knife was shorter than a pin but very sharp, and Colin managed to cut two openings for the pilots to see through.

"Super," said Drogel.

The three left the room. They made their way stealthily down the carpeted hallway, taking a path which would avoid the elevator. Soon, they reached a door that had the word EXIT written above it. Colin looked over his shoulder. No one was in sight. He pushed open the metal door and was about to take the first step down a long flight of stairs when—

He saw someone standing in the corner. Crazy Rick!

"Hah! Trying to sneak out, eh, Colin? You thought you could trick me by taking the stairs! You should have taken the elevator! Back to your room! You must rest!"

"I'm not staying here all afternoon!" Drogel said when they were back in their room. "There are two ways down to the lobby, and there is only one Crazy Rick. I think we should try again. Space pilots never give up!"

"They certainly don't," Snogel agreed.

"Let's try the elevator," suggested Colin.

"Right. The elevator is the obvious choice," said Drogel. "It can't fail."

This time they succeeded in reaching the main lobby of the hotel, and off they went onto the streets of San Francisco.

The best way to see a city is to amble around without any set destination. The tours simply are not any good, because they take you only to the large tourist attractions that are bound to be crammed with souvenir shops. Colin knew this, and the three adventurers merely traveled up and down streets at random. They had an absolutely marvelous time. The big city was thrilling to Colin and Snogel and Drogel, and the three had a very difficult job forcing themselves back to the hotel to meet Crazy Rick for dinner at six thirty. He hadn't the slightest idea that Colin had been out of his room for more than three hours.

The National Championship

After breakfast the next morning, Colin walked into the conference hall of the hotel with Crazy Rick. People were rushing about, making preparations for the competition. They were arranging chairs and climbing up ladders and taping wires to the floor and shouting at one another, often in angry voices. And in the middle of the enormous room was a man standing beside a long table, fiddling with a microphone.

"Hey, Jack!" yelled the microphone man, whose name was Ken. "Come over here and give me a hand. I can't get this darn thing to work!"

"I won't be able to help you on that one," Jack answered, carrying two chairs across the room. "I don't know the first thing about that kind of stuff. Ask Harry; he'll know."

"I'm busy right now, Ken," Harry shouted. He was standing on a ladder, screwing a bulb into a spotlight on the ceiling.

"Then how the heck am I supposed to get this sucker to work?" shrieked Ken, turning red in the face.

"Ask Fred," Harry said. "He's a genius with electricity."

"Fantastic!" said Ken. "Where's Fred?"

"He's on coffee break," someone shouted.

"At nine in the morning?" Ken screamed. "He's fired!"

As Colin stood watching this scene of absolute madness, Crazy Rick went off to find the head judge. And at that moment, a boy about fourteen years old poked his head through the doorway, looked around, and saw Colin. He watched Colin for a couple of seconds as if he were trying to remember something and then approached him slowly.

"I know you," the teenager said. "You're Colin Filmore, the guy who scored over a million points at the Regional Championship. I saw you on the cover of some magazine. I'm competing in this contest, too. My name's Doug."

"Hi," Colin said. The two shook hands.

"Before I read about you, I thought I was good. The scores you get make me look like a beginner. It must have taken you a long time to become as good as you are."

Colin laughed, uncomfortable.

"The rest of us don't stand a chance against you," Doug said. "But there's always second and third place," he added cheerfully. "Well, I have to go and eat some breakfast before the contest starts. See you later."

" 'Bye," Colin said.

Crazy Rick came prancing toward Colin. He looked extremely pleased with himself.

"Son, do you have even the slightest idea of what the grand prize is for this contest? I didn't think so. The grand prize is ten thousand dollars! And that, my boy,

is not all. You also win a trip for two to Hawaii! Can you believe it?"

"That's really incredible," Colin said, but suddenly he no longer felt excited. He walked away from Crazy Rick and sat down on a chair. What Doug had said made him feel bad. Maybe using Snogel and Drogel to win the contests had been like cheating. Yes, he decided, it had definitely been cheating. And it would certainly be wrong to win this contest as well. Doug and all the other competitors really worked at the game. He didn't. Then, all at once, he knew what he would do. He felt better immediately.

"Did you hear what Crazy Rick said about the prize?" Snogel asked Drogel from inside Colin's shirt pocket. "It's ten thousand dollars and a free trip to the tropics! We are going to be *terribly* well off after this!"

"I've done it!" Ken cried, clapping his hands together. "I've fixed the mike! Watch this, everybody!" He flipped a little switch, and the microphone promptly burst into flames.

"Get me Harry!" Ken screamed. "Tell him to come here at once!"

"He's gone home," someone said.

"Fred?" Ken asked hopefully. "Is Fred here?"

"He's in the bar, but you fired him, remember?"

"I'm giving him his job back. With a juicy raise. Just get him!"

All the chairs (there must have been close to five hundred of them) had been arranged to form a huge circle. In the middle was a raised platform where two Meteoroids games were placed back to back with a small gap in between. Beside the platform was the long table with the broken microphone.

People were flooding into the hall now. Reporters

poured through the wide doors carrying notebooks or small tape recorders. The reporters were followed by the photographers, who clutched expensive Japanese cameras in their hands. Then came the spectators. All the contestants had arrived earlier.

"Where's Fred?" wailed Ken. "The contest is about to begin, and the mike hasn't been fixed yet!"

"There he is!" Jack shouted.

Through the door stumbled Fred.

Ken started to pray aloud.

"What's the trouble, Kenny?" Fred asked, slurring his words. "The microphone? No problem." He took a screwdriver from the tool belt around his waist and squinted at the mike.

"For heaven's sake, be careful," whimpered Ken. "Is this thing unplugged?"

"Ah-ha!" exclaimed Fred. "I see what your problem is."

Ken waited for Fred to tell him what his problem was. Fred was busy watching a fly crawl across the table.

"Well?" Ken growled.

"What?" Fred said.

"What's wrong with the mike?" shouted Ken.

"Ah-ha!" said Fred again. "You have your wires crossed."

"Great!" Ken yelled. "Super! Now, will you kindly uncross them?"

Fred uncrossed the wires.

"Are you done?" Ken asked.

Fred nodded.

"You're fired."

Five minutes later, Colin was sitting in his assigned seat, listening to the head judge.

"Two contestants at a time will come up to the platform and play. Please notice that the game on my left has a number one painted on its side, and the game on my right has a number two painted on it. When you are called up, make sure that you go to your assigned machine. The time limit is half an hour. A buzzer will mark the end of your turn. When you hear this buzzer, you must take your hands off the controls at once and move back from the game so that a judge can see the score. There will be a short break for lunch in the dining room at twelve, and the contest should be completed by three o'clock. Are there any questions from the competitors? Good. Then I will ask Ian Jacobs and Alex Bateman to start. Ian, on number one; Alex, on number two."

Cameras clicked as they walked up to the games. The main lights dimmed, and the spotlights played brightly on the platform. The head judge shouted "Go," and the two teenaged boys pressed their START buttons. Half an hour passed. The buzzer buzzed. Their scores were called out to the audience.

"Next, we have Doug Baillie on one, and Ranald Boxworthy on two."

Ranald Boxworthy was not a teenager. He was a thirty-year-old man, a millionaire who lived in a luxurious penthouse apartment surrounded by expensive toys. He could easily afford to spend twenty dollars a day on video games.

Mr. Boxworthy did very well, but Crazy Rick was not in the least impressed. He was sitting in the back row of chairs, laughing to himself, thinking that Colin would get a score that tripled or, more likely, quadrupled Ranald Boxworthy's.

"Number one, Charlie Maxwell; number two . . . Colin Filmore."

92

Inside Colin's shirt pocket, Snogel and Drogel were ready, waiting for the boy's hand to slip through the opening, waiting to jump onto it, waiting to be lowered to the floor and to speed into the Meteoroids game. They waited two seconds, then two more. Nothing happened!

As Colin stood up and headed for the platform, everyone in the gigantic audience fell silent. Everyone except Crazy Rick.

"Wipe 'em out, kid!" he bellowed. "Annihilate 'em! Mow them . . ." Rick's voice trailed off as hundreds of annoyed heads turned to look at him. He sunk down in his seat, and his face turned the same color as his beanie.

"Holy horangulodillus!" hissed Snogel, wringing his hands. "He's forgotten to let us out! We're fixed!"

"On your marks!" the judge shouted.

Colin took a deep breath.

"Get set . . . Go!"

And Colin pressed the START button and began to play, by himself, without Snogel and Drogel. He lasted only twelve minutes and scored forty-five thousand points. It was the best he had ever done by himself. It was also the lowest score in the contest.

As Colin walked away from the game, and his score was called out, the people in the audience gasped. They choked. They spluttered and blinked. The reporters' pencils fell out of their hands and clinked on the floor. The photographers' flashes flashed accidentally. Crazy Rick's face was contorted in absolute agony. Colin sat down and began addressing a postcard he had found in his hotel room.

The National Meteoroids Championship was won by Mr. Ranald Boxworthy.

15

Drogel's Brilliant Idea

"He's still sulking," Drogel said to Colin. It was two days after the contest in San Francisco. Colin had just come home from school. "I have never known a person with such capacity for sulking!"

Snogel was sitting very still on Colin's desk, staring out the window.

"How long has he been like this?" Colin asked.

"All day. It's quite appalling. It really is."

"How could you do it to me?" Snogel wailed, beating his fists against the desk. "How could you just throw away ten thousand dollars and a trip to Hawaii?"

Colin watched Snogel, amazed. He found it incredible that such a tiny man could have such an enormous temper.

"We could have been rolling in twenty-dollar bills right now, if it weren't for you!" Snogel cried. "You realize that, don't you?"

"Snogel, I will tell you again what I have been telling you for the last couple of days. It wouldn't have been fair to the others in the competition. We would have been

94

cheating. C-h-e-a-t-i-n-g. It was bad enough winning those first two contests."

"But why, why, why?" moaned Snogel, covering his face with his gloved hands.

"Snogel, stop acting like a child!" Drogel scolded. "I agree with Colin one hundred percent."

Snogel looked at Drogel and Colin through parted fingers. Then he took his hands away from his face. "It's all right now. I'm under control."

"Good," said Colin, "because I have had another brilliant idea. It came to me this afternoon during Mr. Talbot's problems class."

"No way!" shouted Snogel. "You have brought enough misery into my life already. There will be no more brilliant ideas!"

"How is Mr. Talbot?" asked Drogel.

"He's recovering nicely," Colin said.

"That's good. I feel as if I know the man through all you've told us about him. Now, let's hear this new idea of yours."

"No," said Snogel, putting his hands over his ears.

"Snogel, pull yourself together and behave like a proper space pilot. You can at least listen."

"Maybe he doesn't like the idea of making money," Colin said to Drogel.

"That could very well be it," Drogel replied.

"That would be too bad."

"It really would, wouldn't it."

"Cut it out!" said Snogel. "Go ahead and tell me the idea."

"Well," Colin said, "next year, there will be another Meteoroids Championship, and I think I could take away the grand prize *on my own* if you two would train me.

What I mean is that if you could teach me all the strategies you've learned over the years, I could easily become an expert player and—"

"Hold it," said Drogel quietly. "Hold it just one second. I have just had a much better idea." He began scratching his chin gently. "Maybe it's just a bit farfetched. . . ." He was talking to himself now, unaware of everything around him. "Perhaps totally impossible . . . No! No, of course it isn't. It is completely possible!" He looked up at Colin. Drogel's eyes were sparkling in a most unusual way, and there was a strange little smile tugging at the corners of his mouth.

"There is no reason," said Drogel slowly, "why you, Colin, should not become an expert player from *inside* the spaceship! We would, of course, start off slowly by just letting you watch. Then, when you were familiar with the controls, we would let you copilot, and then we would let you pilot the ship all by yourself! That, my dear boy, would be the very best way to become a champion Meteoroids player!"

"Don't be silly, Drogel. It wouldn't work," said Colin. "How would I ever get into the machine?"

"The same way we do, obviously," said Drogel patiently. "The back way is definitely out, it's much too small for a large boy like you, but you could easily enter through the screen."

"Would it work for me, though?" asked Colin, his eyes wide.

"Of course."

"I'm not so sure," said Colin. "I've seen Mr. Schmidt clean the television screen of the game with Windex several times. His hand doesn't disappear into the fantastic level."

kathleen c. howell

"That is simply because Mr. Schmidt hasn't the slightest idea that the fantastic level exists. If he did, his arm would go right through the screen."

"It would give him a heart attack," Snogel said, grinning.

"But I'm so much bigger than you two!" Colin exclaimed. "I wouldn't be able to fit inside the ship. I'd be crushed!"

"Remember, Colin," explained Drogel, "it's a completely different world in there. You'd shrink to the same size as us."

"That's horrible!" the youth said. "How would I explain to my parents how I lost so much weight?"

"And when you left the machine," Drogel went on, "you would return to normal."

Colin was silent for a moment. Then he said, "When would we do this?"

"It would have to be at night," Snogel said, "when there was no one around."

"And on the weekend," Drogel said, "so you could sleep in after the night's work."

"Where?" Colin asked, feeling the old tingling electricity pass through him.

"Crazy Rick's," Drogel said.

"Does it have to be there?" Snogel asked.

"Yes. Now that Mr. Schmidt's closed down. What are you worried about? Crazy Rick won't be around after the amusement center is closed."

"I'm sure he sleeps there," Snogel said.

"Don't be ridiculous."

"Let's try it this Saturday," said Colin.

Diving In

Midnight.

Colin slipped out of bed and closed his door. He was fully dressed. He opened Snogel and Drogel's drawer and saw that they were waiting for him with their helmets on.

"Is it time?" Snogel asked.

"Yes. Let's go."

He put on his jacket and placed the two little men in the pocket they had grown so used to. It was a mild spring night, and as Colin opened his window, a gust of cool air hit him in the face. He ducked out onto the garage roof. Carefully, he walked across it to the tree. Several thick limbs rested against the edge of the roof, and Colin climbed down to the ground.

"Hey," Colin heard a muffled voice say. "Hey, Colin, let us out of here. Nobody's going to see us at this hour. We can walk quite well; we hardly ever trip and fall."

He reached into his pocket, let the two pilots get a grip on his hand, and lowered them to the lawn.

"Come on," he whispered, and the three started toward Crazy Rick's Amusement Center.

"Nervous?" Drogel asked.

"Yes," said Colin. "Very."

The rest of the journey was made in silence. They met no one along the way.

When they had almost reached the amusement center, Drogel said to Colin, "You stay here, out of sight, until we tell you to come."

Drogel and Snogel walked up to the large glass door of the amusement center. Drogel rapped the glass several times. There was no response.

"Maybe they're all asleep," Snogel said.

"Give them a chance," Drogel said, knocking again.

This time, they saw someone walking across the floor toward them. It was a controller. He was dressed in a bright red uniform, and on his head he wore a funny little pointed cap.

"You haven't been locked out by any chance, have you?" he asked, pressing his face against the glass so he could be heard on the other side.

"No," said Drogel, "we don't work here. But could you please let us in? We would like to use a game for a while."

"What game do you control?" the man with the pointed cap asked, looking carefully at Snogel and Drogel.

"Meteoroids," Snogel told him. "Could you please let us in?"

"Certainly. One moment, please," the man said, walking away. When he returned, he was followed by twenty other controllers.

"What's wanted here, Fex?" a controller asked the man with the pointed cap.

"Well, Stu, we want to let those two Meteoroids pilots in, so if you could get to the lock, halfway up the door, that would do the trick."

Stu had a powerful set of suction cups attached to his hands and feet, and he was able to crawl up the glass door very quickly. He turned the large metal knob, unlocking the door, and slid down to the floor.

"That was stupendous, Stu!" said Fex. "Now, let's give this door a good shove!"

All the controllers lined up against the bottom of the door and pushed.

"Let's put some muscle into this!" cried Fex.

Slowly, the great door swung open. A controller carried over a doorstop and shoved it in place under the door.

"Great," said Drogel to Fex. "Now listen, we have a friend with us who will be coming in as well. It might come as a bit of a shock to you all."

"It isn't a Galactic Gunman, is it?" Fex croaked.

"Good heavens, no!" said Snogel.

"Don't panic," said Drogel. He turned and waved at Colin. The boy came out from around the corner and walked to the door.

"Oh, my!" said Fex. "Oh, dear!"

"We're all doomed!" Stu wailed.

"Run for your lives!" screeched someone at the back of the amusement center.

"Do you realize what you have done?" gasped Fex. "You've ruined us. That boy will report us at once. We'll be put in birdcages with newspaper on the bottom!"

"Calm down," said Drogel. "We have known Colin for a long time, and he hasn't told anyone about us. It is perfectly safe."

"Are you certain?"

"Absolutely. May we come in?"

"Well, I guess it will be all right."

Colin walked in after Snogel and Drogel and closed the door. He had to watch his footing carefully. There were so many little men about that he could easily squash one if he were careless. All around him, he felt magic. All the little controllers, some down on the floor, most sitting on game ledges, seemed to twinkle. Even Snogel and Drogel looked different to him.

"What is it you're planning to do tonight?" Fex asked Snogel.

"My companion, Drogel, and I are going to show Colin how to pilot the Meteoroids ship like a master. He's going to watch us fly."

"How nice," said Stu. "He'll enjoy that, watching you from the screen."

"No, you don't quite understand," Drogel said. "He's coming inside to watch us."

"*Inside!*" all the controllers cried.

"Why, it's quite unheard of!" exclaimed Stu.

"Can it even be done?" Fex asked.

"Of course it can be done, man!" cried Drogel.

"There is absolutely no reason why it shouldn't work," Snogel said.

Fex thought about this for a moment. "No," he said, "I suppose there isn't."

"You're making history!" hollered Stu, who was now hanging from the ceiling by his feet. "History!"

"Is there anyone in that Meteoroids game over there?" Snogel inquired.

"No," said a little man dressed like Drogel and Snogel. "My copilot and I are out, and you're welcome to use our game for a while."

"Thank you very much," said Drogel. "Now all we need is someone to press down the START button once we're all inside."

"I'll do it," said Stu.

"Fine! Now, Colin, in you go!"

Colin walked over to the game and slipped a quarter into the coin slot. He stood looking at the dark screen. He wondered whether it really was possible that he could go right through it.

If he believed.

And did he?

To be perfectly honest, yes.

"Do I need a helmet?" Colin asked Snogel.

"Heavens, no!"

"Why are you wearing a helmet then?"

"Simply for effect, my huge boy. Are you ready now?"

"Yes."

"Dive in, Colin!" shouted Drogel.

And he did.